unnerving

twelve unsettling stories plus one

PHOBIA

BLUE FORGE PRESS

Port Orchard ✸ Washington

Unnerving Phobia
Twelve Unsettling Stories Plus One
Copyright 2024
by Blue Forge Press

Cover art by Brianne DiMarco

First Print Edition, September 2024
Second Print Edition, September 2024

ISBN 979-8-89439-019-2

For information about film, reprint or other subsidiary rights, contact: blueforgegroup@gmail.com

Blue Forge Press is the print division of the volunteer-run, federal 501(c)3 nonprofit, Blue Legacy (EIN 83-4307421), founded in 1989 and dedicated to supporting artisans marginalized due to race, age, disability, economics or other factors. We strive to empower storytellers from all walks of life with our four divisions: Blue Forge Press, Blue Forge Films, Blue Forge Gaming, and Blue Forge Sound. Find out more at www.BlueForgeGroup.org

Blue Forge Press
7419 Ebbert Drive Southeast
Port Orchard, Washington 98367
blueforgepress@gmail.com
360-550-2071 ph.txt

*To those who face their fears,
no matter how they manifest—
whether in shadows, silence,
or the depths of their own imagination.*

CONTENT WARNING

This book is intended for mature audiences as these stories are purposefully meant to unsettle the reader. If one month's story is too intense, skip that month. While the editor and Blue Forge Press have selected and edited each of these stories, ultimately you are responsible for curating what you read.

For a full list of triggers by story, please write to:
blueforgepress@gmail.com

table of contents

unnerving

twelve unsettling stories plus one

PHOBIA

January

Survivor's Guilt
Bree Indigo

he president is on tv again
but this time no one mentions
affairs or *that woman*
and his words are familiar
to my ten-year-old mind
       sticks and stones will break my bones
       but words will never hurt me
I don't fully comprehend
the tragedy that occured
    the chaos, confusion
    and bloodshed
or the word that would become
    synonymous with school shooting
    columbine
he is promoting peer mediation as a fix
for the massacre that happened
two days ago in Colorado
oversimplifying dylan and eric's lives
and pacifying the public

with children's rhymes
explaining that words
can and do
        hurt
creating a legacy
of victim blaming
        and mental health scapegoating
while ignoring the truth
        that our great nation
        can't keep its kids
        safe

practicing "lockdown" becomes as regular
as fire and earthquake drills
but we have our first real lockdown
that same year
        when an armed robbery suspect
        cuts through our school campus
        with the Everett police
        (also armed)
        in pursuit

more than a dozen years pass
and I'm backstage
        at the ballet winter showcase
when we learn what happened
at Sandy Hook Elementary
        that day

I stay focused on my kiddo
          costume and scene changes
          and med kit close by
                    —just in case
and it isn't until
we get home
that the reality sets in
          a deep, dark, vanta-black pit
          grows in my stomach
sorrow tinged with guilt
that I am here
          watching *Glee* with
          my children
while there are parents
who sent their kids
to school that morning
          and will never see them
          again

six and a half years later
on a Saturday afternoon
I am with my daughter
at our favorite mall
          where all the best stores
          have at least two floors
when we hear
a commotion behind us
loud and frantic
          like a rack of pots and pans
          crashing to the floor

we turn to see
a wave of people
        running, panicked, past us
        and down the stairs
my blood runs cold
        and fills me with
        a strange, hollow calm
I find someone with a nametag
        but they're not sure what's happening
        either, but says they're
        locking down the store
                and we should hide
crouching behind a wall
someone says they heard
someone say there was
        a shooting—outside, maybe?
and the cold in my veins
        c r y s t a l l I z e s
                into shards of ice
                        or glass
everyone is (outwardly) calm
as the moments stretch
and we wait to see
        what will happen net
but then finally
in what could have been
five minutes or fifty
a manager gives the all-clear
and an announcement
comes over the mall's loudspeakers

"There's been a fabricated incident
due to a YouTube celebrity
trying to cause a panic.
Please remain calm."

we were safe that day
     there wasn't a real threat
     just a glimpse of what could be
and what did happen
     last year
     (more than once)
at that same mall, only
this time, we weren't there
     but someone else's daughter was
     and she never went home to her mom
         or her family
     she'll never have another birthday
         or graduate nursing school
         and create a family of her own
     instead, she's forever seventeen
     frozen in time
     loved and missed
         but gone
a quarter century has passed
     since Columbine
but the rhetoric remains the same
     we offer *thoughts and prayers*
         and hope it doesn't happen again
         and again and again
     while changing nothing and
     fulfilling the definition of insanity

but we are told that
    we can't live in fear
so we go out
    to the movies
        and try not to think about
        the Dark Knight
    to Wal-Mart
        and try to forget
        the shootings that happened
        at our local store
    to video game competitions
    at Mandalay Bay
        with brand new metal detectors
and we teach our high schoolers
    how to play dead
    fake blood capsules
        in their mouths
    and teflon shields
        in their backpacks
while we argue about gun control on facebook
    as if Australia hasn't already shown
        that mass shootings can be
        nearly entirely prevented
            by outlawing semi-auto
        and automatic firearms
    as if the numbers are lying
        that seventy-seven percent
        of mass shooters kill
            with legally purchased firearms

and our inability
to take action
guarantees
        we will always
        live in fear

there were more mass shootings in 2023
in the United States
        than days in the year
how many will
this new year
bring?

february

The House

Dakoda Foxx

In a small town called Flond lived a cheerful couple—Peggie and Delia. Peggie was tall, around 6'2", with a size 12 boot. She looked like she could take out the whole football team if she wanted to. Delia, on the other hand, had a small frame and wore a size six shoe, but her sharp mind and quick wit made up for it. Together, they were an unstoppable force, and after three years, they had become inseparable.

Peggie was turning 25 on February 15th, a date that marked not only her birthday but the day she and Delia had met. Delia wanted to make this year special, so she decided to take Peggie fishing for her birthday. They were also going to spend Valentine's Day weekend in a lakeside cabin in Kentwood.

Delia's father, Karl, had rented a truck for them to make the trip up the mountains. "Be ready to go and pack your bags!" Delia had told her excitedly. "I'm taking you on an adventure."

Peggie hadn't been fishing since she was little, and the idea of the trip filled her with excitement. Her father had been in the military, and after years of moving around, they had settled in Flond. Now, the thought of revisiting a favorite childhood pastime made her giddy.

As they packed up the truck, Peggie asked, "Do we have everything?"

Delia checked over their gear. "Yeah, we're good. Let's hit the road."

Delia and Peggie laughed and sang as they drove up the mountain, the truck bouncing along the winding roads. The air grew cooler, the trees denser. But as they got closer to the cabin, the lighthearted mood began to shift.

"Hey, did you see that sign back there?" Peggie asked, a nervous edge creeping into her voice.

Delia glanced over. "Probably just a local trying to scare people off. Don't worry about it."

Peggie, not entirely convinced, added, "I hope so. You said you checked this place out, right? It's safe?"

"Totally," Delia said, trying to brush off Peggie's concern. "Let's not freak ourselves out before we even get there."

But as they pulled up to the cabin, both of them felt a sudden jolt of discomfort. The cabin looked nothing like the picture from the website. The gate was rusted and barely standing. The grass was overgrown, reaching nearly to their knees. The house itself had a dull, faded look, not the charming getaway they'd expected.

"Okay... something's off here," Peggie said, holding up the brochure. The two stood in silence, the unsettling quiet around them pressing in. No birds. No rustling leaves. Just stillness.

"Delia! Delia!" Peggie shouted from the other side of the truck.

"What is it?" Delia asked as she jogged over.

"Isn't that where we were supposed to go fishing?" Peggie pointed toward the lake.

Delia froze. The lake was completely dried up, a ghostly boat leaning awkwardly in the middle of what used to be water. The pier was broken, its remains sticking out of the ground like skeletal fingers. But what caught Delia's eye was the ground itself—it was bright orange, with a strange, glittery substance coating it.

"How is this possible?" Delia muttered, her mind racing.

Peggie's voice cut through the stillness. "Well, I know what's not happening—me fishing."

Delia looked around, unsettled. "It's late. Maybe we can leave in the morning."

Peggie shook her head. "Orange glitter lake, run-down house, creepy fence? Nope. I don't care how long it takes—we're leaving now."

Delia walked toward the house, determined to make the best of it. The screen door hung loosely, half off its hinges. She found the key under the frog statue, just like the owner had said, but when she tried the doorknob, it came off in her hand.

"Peggie, come on, let's just check inside. Maybe the inside's better than the outside."

Peggie stayed by the truck, her eyes darting nervously around. "I'll wait out here, thanks."

Delia stepped inside, immediately hit by the musty smell of neglect. The place was a disaster. A refrigerator hung halfway open, and the same glittery orange dirt they'd seen at the lake covered the kitchen floor.

"There's something seriously wrong with this place," Delia whispered, glancing nervously toward the stairs. But before she could investigate further, Peggie's panicked voice echoed from outside.

"Delia! That rope—it's moving by itself!"

Delia ran out to see what Peggie was talking about. Sure enough, a rope hanging from a nearby tree was swaying in the still air, as if being tugged by some unseen force.

"There's no wind," Peggie said, wide-eyed. "That shouldn't be happening."

Delia sighed, trying to keep calm. "Let's just go inside and sleep. We'll leave at first light."

"No way," Peggie said, but before she could argue further, a strange thumping noise echoed from upstairs.

"What was that?" Delia asked.

Peggie paled. "I don't care. Let's go."

But Delia's curiosity got the best of her. "Let me check. Stay here."

Peggie stayed frozen near the truck, and that's when she saw it—spiders, dozens of them, crawling over the truck's windows. Her fear kicked in, and without thinking, she tore off her shirt and threw it on the ground, flailing to shake them off.

Delia rushed back outside to find Peggie half-dressed and in full panic mode. "Peggie, what are you doing?!"

"I don't want anything for them to hang onto!" Peggie yelled, frantically trying to get rid of the invisible spiders she thought were on her.

Delia tried to keep it together. "You know they can crawl on you whether you have clothes on or not, right?"

That didn't help. Peggie screamed, "Let's go, Delia! I'm serious! I don't care if we have to drive all night!"

Suddenly, the house behind them groaned, a deep, rumbling sound. The ground shook as the house began to lift itself off the ground—on massive spider-like legs.

Delia's breath caught in her throat. "Peggie, get in the truck. Now."

They ran for the truck, but it was covered in spiders. Delia didn't mention that to Peggie as she jumped inside and started the engine.

The truck swerved down the dirt road, the windshield wipers barely clearing the swarm of spiders crawling over the glass. The house behind them moved with a terrifying speed, its legs clattering like firecrackers hitting the ground.

Peggie, now hyperventilating, yelled, "Why does it have to be spiders?! I'm terrified of spiders!"

"I don't know, Peggie! I'm driving as fast as I can, but that thing is right behind us!" Delia shouted over the noise.

As they reached the main road, the spiders on the windshield turned into glittery orange dirt, scattering into the wind.

Peggie, her voice shaking, pondered aloud, "Am I dreaming? This can't be real."

"If you're dreaming, I'm dreaming too," Delia replied, gripping the steering wheel, her eyes fixed on the road ahead.

The house stopped at the edge of the town, watching them disappear into the distance. The further they drove, the quieter it became.

Soon Delia and Peggie found themselves pulling into Delia's parents' driveway. They jumped out, running to the front door. "Mom, Dad, we need help!" Delia yelled.

Delia's father, Karl, stepped outside, staring at the orange dust covering them. "What in the world happened to you two?"

"Spiders, Dad," Delia said breathlessly. "And a house—a house with legs—it's chasing us."

Karl blinked. "A house with legs? You sure you didn't hit your head out there?"

"I'm telling you, it's real!" Delia said, her voice sharp with urgency. "The spiders, the house—everything. We barely got away."

Peggie, still jittery, grabbed Karl's arm. "Please tell me you have something to kill spiders. I can't handle this anymore."

Karl, seeing the panic in Peggie's eyes, decided not to press for more details. "Alright, alright. Come inside. We'll figure this out."

They followed Karl inside, where Delia's mom, Amy, was already pulling supplies out of a cabinet. "What in the world is going on?" she asked, glancing at Peggie, who still looked ready to bolt at the slightest movement.

"We don't have time to explain everything," Delia said, pacing near the door. "We have to leave Kentwood, now. There's something seriously wrong up there, and we can't stay."

Amy, sensing the tension, nodded. "Alright, let's get moving. Where are we going?"

"We need to get far away from that place. I don't even know how to explain it all, but trust me, you'll understand if you see it," Delia replied.

Karl grabbed his keys and a duffle bag. "Let's get some supplies first. We're gonna need food and weapons."

Amy, now visibly concerned, turned to Delia and asked, "Is this about Rodney? Is he back again, bothering you two?"

Delia sighed. "No, Mom, it's not Rodney. I wish it were that simple. It's... spiders. And a house that was chasing us."

Peggie, still pacing near the truck, chimed in, "And that house was massive! I swear, if I see one more spider..."

The group piled into the truck, Karl sitting in the back with a shotgun resting across his lap, ready for whatever might come. Delia drove, her eyes flicking nervously to the rearview mirror, half-expecting to see the house reappear at any moment.

They stopped at a small store on the way out of town, the sky growing darker overhead. As they pulled into the parking lot, the man behind the counter watched them closely, his eyes narrowing as they stepped out of the truck.

"You folks just come from Kentwood?" he asked, pointing to the orange dust on their clothes.

Delia exchanged a glance with Peggie. "Yeah. Why?"

The man wiped his hands on a rag, leaning over the counter. "We've had a few people come through here looking like you do—covered in that orange dirt. Seems like something strange is going on up there."

"No kidding," Peggie muttered, still on edge. "We barely got out."

The man nodded gravely. "Whatever's up there, it can't come across the bridge. You're safe here."

Delia let out a breath she didn't realize she was holding. "So it won't follow us?"

The man shook his head. "Not as long as you stay this side of the bridge."

Amy, overhearing, grabbed a few more supplies from the shelves. "I don't like the sound of this one bit. We need to hurry."

Before they left, the gas station attendant caught Delia's arm. "You're going to need this," he said quietly, handing her a small box. "It's protection. Use it wisely—you only get five of them."

Delia opened the box to find small, metallic tokens.

"What are these?"

"They'll keep you safe, but only if you use them when the house passes the bridge. If it comes for you again, you'll know. And watch out for the monkey clown—it can change the scenery on you. Don't get lost."

Delia's brow furrowed. "Monkey clown? What in the world are you talking about?"

The man just shook his head. "You'll see. Good luck."

They hurried back to the truck, the weight of the tokens heavy in Delia's hand. As they drove away, she kept glancing back at the small town of Flond, wondering if they had truly escaped or if the strange nightmare had only just begun.

In the truck, Peggie sat with her arms wrapped around herself, staring out the window. "I'm not going back there, Delia. Ever."

"We won't," Delia said, gripping the steering wheel. "But we need to figure out what's going on."

Karl, still keeping an eye on the road behind them, leaned forward. "What's the plan now?"

"We head toward Rice," Delia said. "The guy at the gas station said it's safe there, too."

Peggie glanced back at the disappearing road. "And what about the spiders? The house? What if it catches up?"

"We'll deal with it if it happens," Delia replied, her

tone steady but uncertain. "We just need to keep moving."

As they drove further away from Kentwood, the eerie feeling began to fade, but the memory of the house and the spiders lingered. They had made it across the bridge, but something told Delia that this wasn't over. Not yet.

MARCH

Shot by the Arrow of Time
Pauline Ugalde

1.

I bend down and pluck the razor blade free of its hiding spot, wedged between the floorboards—one last, futile effort to debilitate me, even from beyond the grave. He wanted me to bleed out.

Of course, I know him well enough to avoid it. He knew that I wouldn't die. He knew I'd find it, but he wanted to plant it anyway; a desperate act to reclaim his sense of control.

I sit at his bedside, my extended index and middle fingers pressed against the inner portion of his wrist to check his pulse. Indeed, he'd died within the last twenty minutes. The mattress and sheets still hold his residual body heat. "But you didn't double-tap yourself soon enough," I clarify to no one.

I close his eyes but otherwise waste no time. I raise

my arms, eyes intent on the floor below me, and produce a flask from my belt, positioned so it hovers in front of me. Strained creaking noises, then resounding cracks and screeches, echo throughout the empty house, upending the floor. Still, I remain unphased and upright as the floorboards, then furniture, orbit around me. I splay my fingers and lower my arms to chest height, making motions like separating pebbles from fine sand.

Just as I anticipated, the objects grow clean once more, the blood coating them flowing downward into the flask. The room overturned in every way around me, I kneel next to his bed. Hands wrist-deep in the beaker, I paint blood on his wounds, outline his heart on his chest, the paths of his major veins and arteries, and standard electrode positions on his skull. With what remains, I dab his own blood on his eyelids and submerge the pendant around my neck.

Time doesn't rewind like a film or recalling a memory. Events neither undo themselves in one smooth motion, nor objects revert to their prior states without errors. Reversing entropy isn't easy. It grows harder the more disordered a system is, in fact. Still, nothing can resist: Not the carbon nanostructures in the walls, not the transparent, aluminum windows, not the AI planted in every surface, just as befuddled and fearful of death as their owner.

No.

Reality at all levels of scope begs for death, but I refuse to comply. Instead, I toy with the ultra-advanced materials around me, every square foot worth more money than ninety-nine percent of people will make in a year. This house means nothing to me.

Only his life does. Only he does. Only what he feels matters.

Cyrus wakes up, all according to plan. I reposition myself at the opposite end of the grounds, just off the property—not at his bedside, like last time.

Let him believe that he's won again, that he's triumphed again. Let him believe that he's driven me away. Let him believe that his precious innovations, his desire to cheat death, have silenced me.

He's wrong. He's wrong. He's wrong.

2.

I wake with a gasp.

It takes only a second for me to realize two things. The first is that I'm on the floor, my sheets tangled around my body.

The second is that I'm awake at all.

I burst into tears. *I double-tapped myself. But I failed. Again.*

I bury my head in my folded arms, even though my pillow is mere feet away, and sob, silk thread be damned, my throat growing raw after... a couple minutes? Hours? This doesn't last, however. I return to lying on my back, crying without muffling my voice whatsoever.

He already knows how I behave. He always finds me.

He likes—

No.

He loves the struggle. I always cry out in pain. Why wouldn't I? No matter how many times I live through this, the pain feels equally real.

The implant in my ear speaks in a facsimile of a soft, calm, soothing tone, responding to my distress. I stopped listening to it years—

No.

To the outside world, I've only spent one day here. To me, it feels like years instead.

Resigned, I rise from bed. My morning routine comes to me by muscle memory, even shaving my face. I flush the casing for the disposable razor blade down the toilet and slip the blade itself into my sleeve. Its cold, reassuring profile lies flush against my forearm. The speaker in my ceiling plays soft piano music, using vintage samples, overlaid with a flute. Panoramic, 3D, global scenes flow across my walls and ceiling: California's Humboldt Redwoods State Park, Germany's Black Forest National Park, and Yemen's Dragon's Blood Forest. Interspersed between the frames are closeups of my parents—at peak health and at the moment of their deaths. Slashes mar their throats, then vitreous fluid pools under their empty eye sockets, then flames engulf them, burning them almost beyond recognition.

Only when I'm fully dressed, my father's pendant resting against the collar of my black shirt, and sitting in front of my TV, do the visuals transfer over to the walls of my room. I unseal the display cabinet for the console, game, and controller. Its weight calms me down, if only slightly. Out of habit, I gently blow on the gaming console's cartridge before inserting it. As the game boots up, I reach into the back of the same cabinet, flipping a set of switches and completing multiple biometric scans. Gaspar's voice in my ear, simultaneously alien and familiar, responds to the new inputs: "Take care of yourself. I'll be here if you need me."

I hum along to the title screen, but my attention focuses forward, to my next set of party members, my next bracket of self-imposed challenges. *I've played Chrono Trigger once a year since it came out. Even last year. Not even death stopped me from playing this, you bastard.*

I settle into my spot on the floor, glancing behind me at the flickering images of my parents on my back wall. Gaspar speaks using replications of their voices, gathered from lifetimes of recordings, and makes gestures taken from analyses of their body language.

If I'm fast, I'll defeat Lavos before...

No.

I will defeat Lavos today. I always have. This sadistic fuck won't change that.

3.

I don't even need to hack his security cameras. I already know that he woke up a few minutes ago. I don't need to scramble his at-home internet of things network with false data, or even garrote the employees—

No.

I leave everyone else on the grounds untouched. They work here for the pay, not him. Why would they even like him or think of him as a friend? He doesn't do the same for them.

My footsteps ring against marble floors in name only. In reality, they are panels which collect data about the occupants—

No.

Occupant, now.

No.

Gaspar collects data about Cyrus, and no one else—

No.

Gaspar performs these functions for hundreds of wealthy clients worldwide simultaneously. Cyrus announced the project a year ago, in front of hundreds of transfixed stakeholders, reporters, and industry experts. Funding, swift and copious, came soon afterward.

Not even Gaspar—the culmination of generative AI models in fields including, but not limited to, healthcare, career coaching, entertainment, finance, and psychology—is ready for me. Wherever I go, accrued DNA samples from Cyrus' most frequented places on the grounds track onto every surface I touch and glare at. Gaspar obeys me, as effectively as if Cyrus himself gave the orders. They don't even begin expressing a warning when the weight and sheen of the tiles draw my eye. I claw the air with both hands, rending one from the floor, just outside Cyrus' room.

He doesn't even notice me as I deceive Gaspar into unlocking his door. He's too engrossed in his game to care. I walk up behind him.

I bash his skull with the tile.

I don't expect Cyrus to wrestle it away from me.

My concentration immersing the tile, it breaks as he seizes an object—

No.

He seizes a sword from a display on his wall without hesitation, both hands on the hilt. He makes a lunging stab toward my chest, in a confident, grounded stance—

No.

He shouts his defiance, each word paired with a stabbing motion, each faster and more impassioned than the last.

"I! Have! My! Own! Will!"

I don't care.

My initial attack achieved its purpose. The flecks of blood and hair clinging to the floor tile provide just enough information. With full force, I will the tile to redirect at Cyrus' throat—

No.

He drops the sword and wrenches the tile out of the air, shifting his weight. He's poised to impale me with it instead.

Gritting my teeth, I jerk my head back. The tile writhes free of his grip. I slash my index fingers across my throat.

The tile doesn't just sever his jugular artery. It decapitates him, cutting deep and fast enough to touch his spine, and to drench him, down to his black dress pants and shoes, in blood.

As he collapses, his futile attempts to grab his controller grow weaker by the second. His eyes settle into a wide stare at his TV, displaying the last moments of a boss fight. I stand over him with one foot on his chest. With my free hand, I pull his father's pendant over his head and drape it around my own neck, to complement his mother's.

Repeated jerks of my head shatter Cyrus' sword, then each simulacrum of his parents, then the TV, then his Super Nintendo, then his post-mortem generative AI console.

I accompany each movement with words of unrestrained hatred: "But. The. Future. Refused. To. Change."

aPRIL

When to Go, and When to Stay
Avery Kellam

Chapter 1

Harper

"My mom went out of her way to prove these things existed, to my detriment," I said. "If I can prove they're real, maybe she'll come back."

"She's not coming back," he said, and I almost slapped him. "She's dead. You saw her body. She's buried and is now resting quietly in Holy Name."

"But she's not," I said. "Trust me when I tell you that she's roaming that place every day. She can't rest until I can prove these things exist."

"So, you believe in ghosts but not cryptids?" he asked, and the sarcasm dripped from each word.

"Look," I said. "I know my mom. She'd want an answer. I want to give that to her."

"What if you prove they don't exist?" he asked.

"You know you can't prove a negative, right?" I asked.

"You could still be attacked by a person," he said. "Or by wild animals. Either of those options will still end up with you dead."

"You're being dumb," I said. "And I'm perfectly capable of taking care of myself."

"Look," he said. "I've put up with a lot of shit from you over the last four years with your back and forth with your fucking mom. If anything, I'm surprised you aren't *glad* she's dead. Like, what the fuck? Why are you so invested in her bullshit? Seriously. Okay, so the monsters are real. Everyone fucking knows that, Harper. Your mom was batshit crazy and went out into the woods and got herself killed, and you're going out there to do what? The same fucking thing? And for why? You didn't even like the bitch, anyway."

"Reuben," I said, but he pressed on.

"I'm sick of this," he said. "I'm sick of you. It's like you've lost your goddamn mind this last year. You're not even fucking around anymore. It's like I'm living with a ghost. Your mom is dead, Harper. Six feet under. And she isn't coming back. She's finally at peace, and you need to let this whole thing die with her."

"How fucking dare you?" I asked. "You didn't like my mom, but you're fine with staying in her house now that it's mine. God, my dad never did like you, and now I see why. Maybe I should have thrown you out a long time ago, but I thought you actually cared about me. Thought maybe I found someone who understood what I was going through. Instead, I get a fucking asshole who I wouldn't piss on if he was on fire."

"She got your dad killed," he said. "Doesn't that say something? Shouldn't you be pissed off about that?"

"My dad died doing what he always promised me he'd do," I shouted. "Protecting 'his girls', which included my mom—he loved her, and he loved me, and he died for what he loved—don't you even *dare* think to bring up my dad after what you just said about my mom."

When I found her journals, I was floored. She'd been hunting cryptids her entire life. It was like she was on that television show about the hunters taking them out. I'd always thought the show was kooky and off beat, never that it could actually happen. The fact that my mother was a real-life hunter, someone who went after the monsters, didn't sit well with me... it explained a lot, though.

I was reading the notebook from when I was about seven, and the things she wrote in there were terrifying. Dad had wanted her to stop, to stay home and take care of me, but she was determined to find answers. When she said she was working, she was really out there hunting down these invisible creatures that didn't really exist.

My dad was the one who kept me grounded, made sure I had a normal upbringing, and didn't get pulled into my mom's delusions. I mean, he loved her with everything he had, but he knew she wasn't gonna stop until she proved it. She never tried to take me with her on any of her hunting trips, but I did notice her absence. Dad did his best to not badmouth her, coming up with excuses as to why she missed major milestones for me. After a while, I just stopped expecting her to come home.

Now that I'd read her journals, I wondered why Dad hadn't had her institutionalized. She was clearly not right in the head, judging by the things in her book. It would have made things a whole lot easier. But he didn't, and I would never be able to ask him why. They were entombed side by side, in death as they'd been in marriage. I had to figure out what had actually happened to them.

"What are you thinking?" he asked.

"About the fact that I'm done," I said. "I've had enough of your bullshit, and I want you out."

"You're making a mistake," he said.

"Excuse me?" I asked. "What did you just say?"

"That you're making a mistake," he repeated. "You need me to keep your crazy ass safe. Same way your mom needed your dad. She was fucking nuts and should have been in the loony bin, safe from the rest of the world instead of out there, running around doing God knows what, putting everyone around her in danger. You're lucky she's dead, because if she weren't, you'd probably end up just like her."

"Fuck you," I shouted. "I don't give a rat's ass if my relationship with my mother was unconventional, or if my parents relationship wasn't *normal*. I'm sorry it wasn't convenient for you that I didn't have parents who were cookie cutters of the Cleavers. She was my *mother*. What the fuck are you going on about, Reuben? Who actually talks to someone they're supposed to love like that? How can you even say shit like this to me?"

"I'm trying to give you a reality check," he said, still pretending that the shit he'd been saying wasn't horrible.

"Well," I said, walking over to the front door. "Here's your reality check. Get out."

He stood there, not moving.

"Now," I shouted. "Right the fuck now. Get out of my house and while I'm gone, get your shit out, too. I don't want to come back here and see any trace of you left. Oh, and by the way, if you trash my place, I'll call the cops. Yeah, that's right. I have cameras you don't know about all over the place. One of those things my parents had installed when I was young."

"What?" he gasped, his eyes wide.

"Oh yeah," I said. "That means I know what you've been up to when you thought I wasn't around. That bitch ever sets foot in my house again, and I'll call the cops on her, too."

I hadn't actually seen anything, and the cameras were not the best, but I knew he'd been there with someone, so I pushed it a bit, and as expected, he crumbled like the piece of shit he was.

"I can explain," he began.

"I don't need an explanation," I replied, opening the door. "Get out. Now."

"I can't believe you're actually serious," he said, as if everything I'd already said wasn't crystal clear.

"I am," I said. "Get the fuck out of *my* house."

"Fine," he said, stomping over to the door after picking up his jacket. "But we're not over. Not by a long shot."

"Oh, we're over," I said. "If I come home and one thing that isn't yours is gone, you *will* be brought up on charges. And if your shit is here when I get back, I'm burning it. Now, go."

I shut the door in his face as soon as he was out. Was it petty? Sure. But I was done having a conversation he wasn't willing to listen to. I had my reasons, and they made sense to me. I needed answers, and I was gonna get them, even if it killed me.

"Oh, God," I whispered, turning to see the wedding picture of my parents. "What happened to you?"

Chapter 2

Braxton

She was running, frantically through the woods, and it was after her. I hadn't seen this one before, but I knew the type, and they were not safe. I needed to stop her from getting into the woods. But I didn't even know her. She wasn't someone from town, that's for sure. How was I supposed to save someone I didn't know?

I bolted upright in bed, covered in sweat, gasping. It happened every time I had a vision, a glimpse into the future. This one was different, though. This was something I could change, could stop, if I could just figure out who she was, and where the vision took place.

Running a hand down my face, I flipped the covers off me, and headed into the bathroom to take a shower. Every one of these things wore me out, and I just had to get myself back into the right frame of mind so I could get through my day.

My gift, fucked up as it was, had helped me keep my home, my business, and all the things I held dear. Well, except my family. No, they disowned me once they realized that I wasn't just pretending. The moment I told them exactly how my dad was gonna get hurt, on the job up in the mountains, they looked at me different. When it came true, they shunned me. Not outside the house, but they didn't really invest in anything that had to do with me.

I was fed, had a roof over my head, but other than that, I was a ghost in the house. No one talked to me. No one cared when I got sick. Absolutely nothing was done to help me get through my visions. The only person who seemed to even care was my best friend, Jim. He was the one who brought me to his home, brought people in from his community, and they helped me to understand the gift I had.

The day I turned eighteen, I walked out of my house to school, and never went back. I'd been secretly taking things from my home that I knew I wanted to keep, and Jim had been holding on to them for me. When I left my house that last day, the only thing I had left that I needed to take was my laptop, and thankfully it fit in my backpack, so I wasn't suspicious at all. Jim's family let me stay with them until I got enough money to get on my feet.

I found a job at the supermarket in the next town over. I'd been working there since I was sixteen, and had saved absolutely everything from that job in an account that Jim's parents set up for me. They were on the account, and I was just a signer on it, but they never touched the money. When I turned eighteen, we went to the bank, closed that account, and I took the money and opened a new one at a different bank, upon their insistence. It was all so weird to have these people who weren't family treat me better than my blood relatives had.

That first time was terrifying, but I got through it by thinking that telling my dad what was going to happen, I would somehow save him. When my mom got the call that he was hurt, she went into a rage at me, blaming me for bringing the devil into her house. That weekend they took me to their church and had the pastor and several other people try to pray the devil out of me. I sort of went along with it, not understanding what was happening. When I saw what the pastor had been doing during his other sessions, I freaked out, wanting to run as far away from there as possible. But at nine, that just wasn't something I could do.

Instead, I turned everything into myself. All the visions I had become bad dreams. The times I was awake when they happened, I turned them into bad headaches. I had an excuse for everything, and it worked. Jim was the only one who knew the truth for a long time. When I was staying at his house, much to my parent's disgust, he asked if he could tell his great granddad. I was hesitant, but he asked if he could phrase it like a hypothetical, so I could see what the answer would be, and that's just what he did.

"Granddad," he'd said. "If someone told you they were having visions, seeing things that hadn't happened yet, or something that had happened, but the person had no way of knowing about it, what would you tell them?"

"You having visions, son?" he'd asked.

"No," he'd said. "We were just talking about things we saw on a show, and wondered whether it might happen in real life. Then, we wanted to know what someone should do if they had that happen to them."

"I see," he'd said, and I wasn't sure if he actually understood the question, or was thinking about the hypothetical. "Well," he continued after a moment's thought. "I'd tell them that they had been given a great gift. That the ancestors had bestowed upon them something that was rare and beautiful. If they had the gift of sight, then they should always try to help those they could, even if it seemed scary or difficult."

"That's what I thought," Jim had said.

"But what if it meant that their family didn't like them anymore?" I'd asked.

"Well," he'd said, thinking again. "I supposed that what someone thinks about you isn't really that important. It's what you think about yourself that matters. Say this person had the sight, but they never told anyone what was going to happen. If they could have prevented a tragedy, wouldn't you feel like you had done the wrong thing?"

"Even if no one believed them?" I'd asked.

"I guess they'd have to weigh who was a safe person to tell," he'd said. "And if that wasn't someone in their family, or in their place of worship, then they may have to find a friend who was willing to keep their secret, at least until they were in a position to be able to get the help they needed."

He'd looked at me as if he knew, but his words were toned in a way that said he understood that I couldn't really tell him anything. From that day on, I spent as much time as I could at Jim's house. I'd gotten the job at the grocery store, but hid it under the guise of doing community projects. My parents weren't too interested in what I was doing, anyway, so I just kept everything secret. I thought about leaving a note, but decided against it. Not wanting my parents to cause any issues, I just walked away and never went back.

Funny thing was, my parents never came looking for me. I mean, if they'd even thought about it, they would have known where I went, but they never came. I continued the last month of my senior year at high school, graduated, and they didn't come. Didn't even bother to hide the fact that they didn't care. It pissed me off for a while, until Jim's mom told me something that made everything clear.

"Your parents weren't there for you," she'd said. "They were glad you were gone. You were their dirty little secret, and now they don't have to pretend any longer. You're better than they are, though, because you actually care. You will miss them, but more you'll miss the parents you should have had. These two were just the biological donators to your existence. They can now pretend you don't exist. When people ask them about you, they'll tell them that you left, you cut them off. They can pretend they tried to find you, but you went to their devil, so they had to let you go. Hell, they may even say you died. It would be easier for them."

She'd been right, too. I ran into them at some point the next year, and they didn't even acknowledge me. It was like they saw right through me, as if I weren't even there. It killed me, but then I realized that they were the ones who gave up on me, not the other way around, so I held my head high and did the same to them they were doing to me. I'd seen them around off and on over the next few years, but each time, they looked older and more broken. I was the strong one, but they were losing themselves.

At some point, my mom came up to me in a store, and I looked at her and asked her who she was. The look on her face when she said she was my mother nearly caught me, but I simply told her that she must have been mistaken, because my parents died when I was eighteen. She slunk off, tears running down her face, and I haven't seen either of them since. It's been nearly a decade since I first walked away, and I have no idea if they are alive or dead.

I got out of the shower, toweled myself off, and pulled on some jeans and a tee shirt. I had to go talk to someone about what I'd seen, because the last time I saw something like that, there were deaths. Several, in fact, and it was horrible. It had been a year, and I didn't want that to happen again, so I needed to do something. I knew Jim would know who I needed to talk to in order to get my answers.

I sent a text to him, letting him know I was on my way over, and that I had another vision like last year. Hopefully, I wouldn't have to wait long once I got there to talk to one of the elders. They were the ones who helped me initially, and were even better after I left my parents' house. It took a while for me to be able to interpret the visions, but they were clear that I was sacred, and they would ensure my safety at any cost.

They'd asked if I was sure I wasn't adopted, but I told them I was a carbon copy of my father, with little bits of my mother's father thrown in. My blond hair and blue eyes came from my father, and my sharp angled jawline came from my grandfather. It was something I had been proud of initially, but once my parents realized my gift, they tried to say that I looked nothing like either of their families, and that I must be some bastardized child that had been switched in the hospital. They never claimed any relation to me from my first vision onward. I honestly would have felt better if I'd been adopted, because then I could pretend that it wasn't my fault, they'd picked the wrong kid.

The drive to the reservation was long, but it was worth it when I pulled into Jim's driveway and saw several of the elders waiting on the porch for me. I knew he'd call them, but I didn't think they'd come out this early. Either way, I was glad they were there, so I climbed out of my truck and headed to the porch.

Chapter 3

Harper

Reuben had been right about it being cold, but there really wasn't much I could do about that. It wasn't my fault that my parents had decided to do this hunting thing during the spring in northern Minnesota. Besides, it might not turn into anything anyway.

"Welcome," the woman behind the counter at the hotel said as I walked in. "You have a reservation? Or are you just hoping to get a room?"

"I have a reservation," I said.

"What's your name, sweetheart?" she asked.

"Harper McCann," I said.

"Now, why does that name sound familiar to me?" she said as she typed on her computer. "Oh, here we are. You're just here the one night?"

"Yeah," I said. "I'm doing some research tomorrow, so will be out in the woods most of the night. I'll be back the day after, though. You have that date on there, too, right?"

"You're doing what in the woods?" she asked, her eyes wide with horror.

"Just research," I said nonchalantly. "No big deal."

"You can't be in the woods at night," she said.

"During the day is fine, but once the sun sets, you need to be back in town."

"You sound like my ex," I said.

"They must have been smart," she replied. "You do know what's out there, right?"

"That's why I'm here," I said. "Look, I'm not interested in a lecture, I just need to get to my room so I can get some sleep before I spend tomorrow doing my research."

"I don't know if I'm comfortable with all this," she said, her hands still on the keyboard.

"Look," I said. "Are you gonna rent me the room or not? Cause, if you're not, I'm gonna find another hotel."

"All right," she said, her fingers working again. "I just don't understand some folks."

The last was muttered under her breath, but I heard her clear as day. Instead of calling her out on her bullshit, though, I just pretended it didn't bother me. In reality, though, the thought that she was concerned did give me a moment of pause. Maybe I shouldn't be doing this. Maybe my parents *were* killed by some crazy monster that lives in the woods. Thing was, I needed to know. I needed answers, and the only way I saw to get them was to go out there and see for myself.

"I'm gonna need your credit card and the information about your car," she said, pointing to a spot on the form she'd printed out.

I handed her my card and she ran it through her

machine, then handed it back to me. I put the car info onto the sheet, then waited while she finished up with my reservation.

"Here you go," she said. "Room number seven. You can move your car down the way and park right in front of it. Should make unloading anything you want to keep safe pretty easy. Here's the information about bears and the like in the area, too. You know, in case you were interested in staying safe while you're here."

"Thanks," I said, taking the key and the pamphlet she handed me.

"Bears aren't the only dangerous things around here," she said. "Something to keep in mind. I'd seriously reconsider being out after dark, though."

"I'll do that," I said, and turned and walked out of the lobby.

Climbing into my car, I set both the key and pamphlet on the passenger seat, then started it up and pulled back to move down the way the receptionist indicated, pulling right up in front of the door marked with a seven. Getting out, I grabbed the key, but left the pamphlet on the seat. I opened the back door and grabbed my bag, before shutting and locking my car.

It was still early enough that I knew I'd need to go out and grab some food. While I got myself settled into the room, I pulled out my phone and sent a text to Reuben to let him know I was here and safe, reminding him to get his shit out of my house. I'd made an appointment with a locksmith to come out a couple of days after I got back to change the locks. I'd toyed with the idea of one of those electronic ones with a keypad, but thought that would be too much trouble, and I didn't need to add to my insanity.

The comforter on the bed looked homemade, which was an interesting choice, but I guess out in the boonies, you do what you want. The bathroom was small, but big enough, and the room had no television, which I thought was odd, but not an absolute deal breaker. I wasn't here to catch up on some show, I was here to get answers.

I put my bag on the bed, then headed back out to my car, pulling out and heading back to the main part of town, small as it was, so I could find something to eat, as well as grab a few bottles of water to take with me on my trek. I also wanted to grab some granola bars and beef jerky, both of which would be good if I needed nourishment. Toilet paper was another thing I'd shove in my bag, just in case I needed to take care of that kind of business while out there.

There was a small family style restaurant on the corner of one of the blocks, and right next to it was a drug store, so I was in luck in that I'd be able to get all my needs taken care of in one spot and not have to go hunting around to find everything.

The bell above the door to the restaurant rang as I entered, but it didn't need to be there. The place was small, and I was greeted by a young woman who said I could sit anywhere I wanted. I walked past a couple of occupied booths until I found one that was empty and clean.

"Here for a visit?" the waitress asked as she set down a menu and a glass of water.

"Research," I replied, this time without elaborating.

"Ah," she said, but that was it. "I'll be back in a minute to get your order."

"Thanks," I replied, picking up the one sheet menu.

It had the normal food that one finds in a dive diner, and I decided to go with the homemade meatloaf, thinking it might remind me of my parents and the dinners we'd had when I was growing up. The waitress took my order, then headed behind the counter to tell the chef before grabbing a glass to fill with soda.

"So," she said when she brought my soda back. "What kind of research are you doing?"

"Nothing big," I said. "Just checking some things my parents talked about."

"Like, what kinda things?" she asked, and it was a bit annoying.

"I'd rather not discuss it," I said.

"Well, why not?"

"Fine," I said. "I'm not at liberty to say."

"Oh, so you're, like a spy or something?"

"I just told you I didn't want to talk about it," I said. "Then, that I can't talk about it. That should tell you that any question you ask isn't going to get an answer."

"Jeez," she said. "You don't have to be so rude; ya know."

"I wasn't rude until you pushed," I reminded her.

She walked away, not even bothering to realize that her actions caused my response. She brought my food out shortly after, and I did a quick inspection to make sure she hadn't spit in anything. It all seemed good, so I dug in.

After my meal, I paid, then headed next door to grab my supplies. I grabbed a couple of larger jugs of water, a pack of toilet paper, three bags of jerky, and a box of granola bars. As I set them down on the counter to pay, the guy behind the register looked up at me.

"Going on a hike?" he asked.

"I might," I said.

"Just make sure you pack out whatever you take in," he said. "Don't need to ruin the place for others."

"I'm well aware of that rule," I said.

"Good," he replied. "You'd be amazed at the crap we find when we do a cleanup of the woods around here. Always during the day, though. You know not to go out at night, right?"

"I've heard," I replied.

"Good," he said. "Would hate to think a pretty girl like you end up eaten or dead."

"Not sure which of those would be worse," I replied with a laugh.

"Yeah, the eaten part," he said. "Worse, you could end up one of them."

"One of them?" I asked.

"Yeah," he said, still scanning my stuff. "You know. *Them.*"

The way he said it was like he didn't want to call whatever it was by their actual name. As if sating it out loud would give it power or something.

"Don't want to do that," I replied.

He told me my total, and I paid with my card, taking the bag he'd put everything into. I'd be keeping the bag to use as my out bag when I was in the woods. It was like everyone around the area was spooked by the thought of this creature. They believed it was real, and feared it. It was good to fear the unknown in some cases. With everything that people were saying, I was beginning to wonder whether this was the best option for me. But I had to know. I had to see it for myself.

Chapter 4

Braxton

You're gonna need more than that," Liwen said.

"It's all I've got," I replied.

"Sounds like a spirit quest is in order," Kinich said.

"That's what I figured," I replied just as the phone rang.

"Be right back," Jim said as he went into the house.

"What all do you know about her?" Liwen asked.

"She's fit," I said. "As in, she was running without really being winded. Long hair, seemed a dark blonde or light brown. Wearing decent clothes for the woods, but didn't have a pack with her, which was concerning."

"Brax," Jim said as he stepped out the door. "I think

we may have found her."

"What?" I asked. "How?"

"Kelly at the motel out off seventy-one," he said. "She had someone check in this afternoon saying she was doing research and was gonna be out in the woods tomorrow overnight."

"That sounds like our girl," Kinich said.

"Maybe," I replied. "This girl didn't seem like she was a research type person, though. There was something familiar about her. Something I can't quite put my finger on."

"Either way, I think some time in the hut might be worth it," Liwen said. "Probably should get to it sooner rather than later, too."

I'd been there most of the day, talking with them, giving them all the information that I could remember from my vision. We'd gone round and round, over all the things I saw, and none of them could make heads or tails of it. I hated going into the hut, though. Not because it was bad, but because it made my visions that much more real. Every time I had something come to me, and I went in to find the answers, I came out exhausted and feeling cursed instead of gifted.

But it always worked. At least to give me the answers I needed. They were right, in that I had to do this. Especially after what happened a year ago. I saw something similar, but didn't come to the tribe with my concerns, and two people had died. If I'd come, maybe we could have saved them.

Maybe they would have been here with us now, instead of gone. No, this was something I needed to do.

"Okay," I said, after thinking about it for entirely too long. "Let's do this."

Liwen got up and shook my hand, then headed down the steps. I got up and followed him, knowing he was the one who would help me get settled. We climbed into my truck and I drove him down the road to the sacred place where I could commune with my own personal guide to get the answers I sought. I'd done it a number of times, and the few times I hadn't, well, they weren't exactly my favorite memories.

Pulling into the driveway, just off the main street, we meandered down first a paved road, then onto gravel, before finally we were on a dirt path that was bumpy and hard to handle in my little beater of a truck. We were well out of the way of civilization, and away from even the prying eyes of the people who wanted to get a glimpse of some sort of ritual. I never liked that aspect of this, and it always felt like I was a dirty outsider whenever we started it, but knowing that I was being taken for the good of the community, helped to ease my concern.

Liwen didn't talk at all on the way, just sat next to me as we made our way into the desolate space where their private connections happened. The first time I'd come, Liwen had been with me as well. He was older now, with his eagle feathers, as he called the gray in his hair, growing long and showing his wisdom, but he was still the same man who had helped me, guided me, on the path to finding my true self.

I remember him telling me my spirit was just born into the wrong body, and that my parent's rejection of me was because they didn't understand. It was why I was so close with Jim growing up, even before my first vision. We were inseparable, even though my parents hated it. When I cried to him the day after my first vision, he understood and brought his community around me. I was thankful I had them, because without them, I likely wouldn't be there at all.

The truck slowed, and I put it in park once we'd stopped, pulling the parking brake so it didn't roll. Liwen stepped from the truck first, and I waited for him to give me the signal to join him. Everything had already been laid out, so they likely knew this would happen. He entered the hut, did what needed to be done to get the space ready for me, then came out and waved me in.

Climbing from the truck, I felt an unease settle on my shoulders. It was as if the weight of this woman's life hung in the balance of what happened inside that small structure. Even though I hadn't prepared for this like I usually did, they knew the urgency, and insisted it happen today. Especially after the call from Kelly. We knew time was of the essence, and the answers I might find could save her life.

Liwen nodded as I stepped up to him in front of the hut. He gave me a nod, pulled the door open, and I slid inside, knowing that the answers may be in my mind, and I had to find them.

Chapter 5

Harper

The bed was lumpy, the noises from the surrounding area were weird, and I didn't sleep worth shit. But, I was up as soon as the sun was, and getting my shit packed up and ready to go on my little quest. Once everything was packed up, I stuffed it all into the trunk of my truck, and headed to the lobby to check out.

"How was your night?" the man behind the desk asked.

"Fine," I lied. "Just checking out. I'll be back tomorrow, probably, so would like to make sure there's a room I can have. Can you check for me?"

"Oh, sure," he said, clacking away on his computer. "Looks like you've got a reservation for tomorrow, so we're all set. Whatcha doing today?"

"Just some research," I said. "Nothing exciting. I've got accommodations for tonight, just not in this area."

"Ah, I see," he said. "You want a receipt?"

"Nah," I replied.

"Could be a tax deduction," he suggested. "You know, since you're here on official business and all."

"I'm using the card that shows all my transactions," I said. "But thanks for thinking of me."

"Sure, sure," he said. "You have a nice day now, ya hear?"

"I hope to," I said, then walked out the door.

I started my truck up and pulled out, heading deeper into the woods, the way that the GPS was directing me. I knew once I got out there, I'd need to switch to the paper map I had, but for now, my phone still had a signal. I'd contemplated getting a satellite phone, but thought the expense seemed ridiculous. Besides, I was sure I wasn't gonna find anything of interest in the woods, so I wasn't too worried.

The area was beautiful, even with the chill in the air. The trees were starting to sprout, and didn't quite look like a spooky horror movie set while driving through. I had been listening to a podcast on the drive from my house, but as I got deeper into the woods, it started to fizzle, so I just shut it off and listened to the sound of my truck running over the road. I had a map to show me exactly where my mom and dad had been, and I had mapped it out the night before, knowing which forest road to take once I got closer.

Thing was, the closer I got, the bigger the pit in my stomach got, and I felt that uneasiness coming up on me. It was the same feeling I had just before I got the news about my parents. I could feel the doom coming about an hour before a police officer showed up at my door. I opened it up and just knew. It was like the whole world closed in on me and I sort of crumpled to the ground. Reuben had been there, but he wasn't there for me, and I hated that I had to end things with him because of it.

It took entirely too long to get to the forest road, and

I thought I'd passed it, until I saw the sign. Turning to the right, I weaved my way into the woods, following the dirt path that had been hewn from the forest, until I got to a place where a gate was across the road. I shut the truck off and got out, walking over to the gate to see if it had a lock, or if I could open it up and drive further. Unfortunately, I was out of luck on that front, so I went back to my truck, grabbed my backpack that I'd set up for my trek, and locked it up tight.

Pulling my pack over my shoulders, I tugged the straps to make it tight, then headed into the woods. I had my mom's notebook, and a map, and was just going to continue on the same path she did, see what she saw, and maybe get an answer to what the actual fuck she was doing out here.

Chapter 6

Braxton

Everything was dark, just the barest of light coming from a lantern up ahead. I walked along, not really with my feet, toward it. I could hear something struggling, a grunting sound, the closer I got.

"Help me!" she screamed, her voice raspy.

I couldn't see her, could only hear the grunting, and her cries. She was sobbing, and saying something I couldn't make out. Moving along the path, I felt skittish, like I didn't want to go further, but I needed to. I had to find out what was happening.

Bursting through the thicket, I saw it. It was on all fours on top of something, and it was rutting, thrusting its hips over and over again.

"Please, oh, God, please!" she cried, and it didn't even phase the beast.

It paused for a moment, turning its head toward me, and I froze. Looking around with blank eyes, hollow holes at the top of its skull. Its mouth agape with nothing inside. It was hideous, terrifying, something that no one should ever have to gaze upon. After a moment, it turned back to its prey, rutting again.

I moved, slowly, around the clearing, trying to see what it was doing. None of it made sense. This thing ate what it caught, so what was it actually doing here? A few final thrusts, and it groaned out, and that's when I realized it was fucking something, or someone.

Pushing up, it reached down and grabbed whatever was on the ground with its boney hand, pulling it up to standing, and that's when I saw her. The woman from earlier. That thing had been raping her. Dragging her along, it walked further in, and she sort of followed without even noticing anything around her. She was sobbing, barely able to keep up with the long legs of the beast.

My vision ended and I screamed.

Chapter 7

Harper

It was starting to get dark, so I pulled out the lantern I'd brought with me. It was the one that my dad had in the garage. I hoped it would be enough to discourage any wild animals, but I had to do this. Today was the anniversary, and I had to find out what killed my parents.

Deeper and deeper I went, and as the underbrush began to get thicker, I hoped I'd be able to find my way back out in the morning. I was sure the sun would be enough to help me figure it out.

There were some sounds from along the edges of the path, really a deer trail more than anything, and I hoped that the critters were the nice kinds, like the ones in the movies that helped the princess with their housework. The thought of it made me giggle, and the woods went quiet. I guess they didn't see my humor, but that was fine. It meant that I wasn't worried that a bear was walking beside me, or the big bad wolf.

I continued on the path, slowly stepping through the shrubbery, squeezing between trees that were entirely too close together, and on into the darkness ahead of me. If I was someone who was easily scared, I might have turned back around. That wasn't me, though. No, I could handle myself, could deal with whatever came at me in these woods. I was sure of it.

Up ahead of me I saw a clearing, and was thankful that I could step out into it and rest from the hard walk I'd had. It was circular almost, just slightly oval, but mostly round. I wondered whether this was where my parents were attacked.

I set the lantern down, placing the pack next to it, and opening it up, I pulled out the notebook my mom had written in. Sitting on the hard earth, I opened up the notebook, its leather creaking as I stretched the binding. I had put a bookmark into the spot where she'd described the area she was going to search.

I was flipping through pages when I heard it. It was just barely there, but it was unusual. It wasn't an actual animal sound, but something deeper, more guttural. I froze, wondering if this was a mistake.

Chapter 8

Braxton

"We have to go, now," I said. "She's in danger. I have to save her."

"You have time," Liwen said. "There is time."

"No," I said, nearly screaming at him. "You didn't see what I did. There's no way she'll survive, and if she does, she'll wish she didn't."

I was shaking, sweating, my whole body vibing on what I'd seen. I had to get to her, had to find that clearing. I was sure I knew where it was, but not positive. I needed my chosen family to help me, and I couldn't wait.

Running to my truck, Liwen followed, and he made it there before me. How, I had no idea, but he did. He was sitting in the passenger seat when I got there. That's when I knew that whatever had talked to me outside the hut wasn't him.

"We have to go," I said, ripping the door open and jumping in.

"I know," Liwen said.

Starting the truck, I slammed it into reverse, releasing the hand brake and backing out and around in the turnaround spot they'd built in up here. It was bumpy and rough, at least until we got to the gravel. By the time we hit the pavement, the sun was coming up. I hadn't noticed it before, but I'd likely spent the entire night In the hut, finding out what was going to happen. Finding the woman I had to save. When we pulled into the drive at Jim's, he came out to see us. The rest of them had gone home, only Liwen staying with me to watch over me as I had my visions.

"Jim," I said, nearly breathless.

"Hey, man," he said, then saw my face. "Come in."

He held the door open, allowing both myself and Liwen into his home.

"There's a clearing," I said. "It's in the middle of the woods, but I'm not sure exactly where."

"Describe it," he said.

With his job working in the forests, he knew them like the back of his hand. I told him what I'd seen, the walk up to the clearing, and the lantern that was there. I didn't tell him everything, because he didn't need to know that. Besides, his kids were there, and it was late enough that they may have been waking up. No one needed to know what I saw.

"Sounds like it's up off forest road out by Beltrami Island," he said. "Hang on, let me grab a map."

He headed back to his room, and came back with one of those elevation maps he used.

"Yeah," he said, folding it out onto the table. "Here," he said as he pointed to a spot near the northern most part of the state. "This road goes back to a locked gate, but if you go past it, there's a good trail for a while, then deer trails throughout the area. If you follow this one, it'll take you to this nice clearing right here. Perfect spot for a picnic."

"This wasn't a picnic," I said, and my tone told him all he needed to know.

"Let's go," he said.

"No," I replied. "You have a family, and they need you. I'm going."

"I will go with you," Liwen said. "As your guide."

"You sure?" I asked, looking at him.

"Let me be your guide," he said, and I understood that he needed to do this, just as much as I did.

"Okay," I said, looking back at Jim. "Can I take that?"

"Let me mark it," he said, reaching over to the kitchen counter and grabbing a highlighter.

He drew along the highway, then off to the forest road, and further toward the clearing.

"It's been a bit since I've been all the way out there," he said. "But I'm sure it's still there. If you follow the path, you'll find it."

"That's what I saw," I said.

"Spirits guide you," he said, pulling me to him for a hug.

"They haven't let me down, yet," I replied, then turned, and headed out the door, Liwen already next to the truck and waiting for me.

Chapter 9

Harper

It's all in your head, I thought as I looked around me.

There wasn't anything that I could make out. Not like you see in the movies where the glowing eyes look at you from behind the trees. No, the forest was eerily quiet. That, somehow, made it even worse. There weren't any insects, no critters scuttling around, nothing moving in the area at all.

Looking at my mom's book, I flipped to the page where she'd journaled about coming up to the forest. She'd mapped it out, and drawn this crazy creature she wanted to find. It was tall and skinny, like skin and bones, and had these super long arms and legs. Its head was larger than it should have been for the size of the body, and the face was awful. There were these gaping holes where the eyes should have been, no nose, and the mouth was full of these sharp teeth. Honestly, it was comical if you looked at it the right way.

There was a crack from behind me, and I turned around, but nothing was there. I picked up my lantern and swung it toward the trees, hoping the light would sort of fall out that way and I'd be able to see further into the trees. Nothing was there, and I convinced myself my mind was just playing tricks on me.

Going back to the notebook, I started reading her words, and felt a chill run up my spine as she talked about it devouring entire bodies without leaving anything behind. I wondered if she actually believed what she wrote, or if it was just some random thing she found in a book somewhere. She was always reading, but wouldn't let me look at anything she had in her private collection. It was weird, but I didn't know any better, so never gave it any consideration until now.

I smelled something, and I couldn't figure out where the stench was coming from. It was like a skunk had pissed on a dead body, and that whole thing had been lit on fire. There wasn't any smoke coming in, but I kept my head on a swivel, looking all around me to see if I could figure out its origin.

The trees behind me moved, and I whipped my head in that direction, but all I saw was the branches swaying.

"It's just the wind," I said to myself, though I wasn't sure I believed it.

Chapter 10
Braxton

"there," Liwen said, pointing to the road that broke off the main one.

Turning right, I followed it back into the woods, continuing on the dirt road until we came upon a car parked at the end.

"Shit," I said, throwing my own truck into park and shutting it off.

"You go," Liwen said. "I have other business to attend to here."

"Keep the keys," I said, handing them to him. "In case I don't come back."

"You will," he said, and his belief in me gave me the boost I needed to get on with this.

I grabbed my flashlight from the back seat, along with my headlamp, pulling my beanie on before strapping the light to my head. I looked around, trying to determine which way she went, and when I saw that the branches to the left of the gate were bent back, I knew where to go.

Just as Jim had said, the path was fairly open for a while, then got smaller, and was simply an animal trail through the woods. I could see the places she'd been, felt her essence along the way, and the closer I got, the more I could sense her. It took time to get used to everything that was going on in my head, but I could see her in the clearing. She was safe, for now.

Chapter 11

Harper

I heard it again, and the smell was getting stronger. This was something I needed to get rid of, so I decided to be the biggest, baddest bitch I could. I stood up to my full five-foot-nothing height and shouted at the top of my lungs.

"Get the fuck away from me!" I yelled. "I've got a bat, and I know how to use it."

That's when I saw it. Exactly as my mom had drawn it. Had to be seven feet tall, at least, and the skin was gray. It looked sickly, like the pictures I saw from the concentration camps during World War II. Thing was, it had nothing on. Like, it was fucking naked as a newborn. But it wasn't a baby. No, this was definitely male, and it was ready to go, if you know what I mean. Cock sitting upright, hands doing that grabbing thing, and the smell was getting worse and worse.

I turned and ran. I didn't grab my lantern, didn't pick up my pack, I just fucking ran, right into the woods, no rhyme or reason as to where I was going. I just knew I had to get away from it. I knew what it wanted, and it wasn't to eat me. No, that fucker was gonna take me any way it could.

Chapter 12

Braxton

"Get the fuck away from me!" she shouted. "I've got a bat, and I know how to use it!"

I followed her voice, knowing now which direction she was. I kept going, my lungs burning with each step, the brambles and brush trying to trip me along the way. I scooted between trees, jumped over fallen logs, and burst out into the clearing to see it standing there in the light of her lantern.

It was on the other side of the light, but I didn't see her. She was running. I knew it. Just like in my first vision. I had to find her, to save her, but I didn't know where she went.

That's when it turned to me, and I froze.

Its eyes were hollow, leering at me without orbs in the sockets. Its mouth was agape, the teeth sticking out every which way. And his manhood was ripe and ready for action, sticking out in front of him. The noise it made was low, then rose to a screeching sound, and I had to put my hands over my ears to fend it off.

When it took a step toward me it stopped, then looked over its shoulder. My guess was that was the way she'd run. I had to get to her, had to find her before it did. But I didn't know what to do.

"Go," Liwen said, shoving me in the back.

I stumbled into the clearing, and he came out of the trees behind me. There was something different about him, but I didn't have time to dissect it. No, I had to go find her. I skirted the clearing, sliding along the trees. The monster's head swinging back and forth, from me, to Liwen, to the woods behind him, then back again.

Liwen threw something at it, and it turned to him. I took that moment to run past it, into the trees, where I thought she had gone. I don't know how long I ran, but I couldn't stop. I had to find her.

Chapter 13

Harper

It was coming after me. I ducked down behind a tree and under a fallen log, the ground soft beneath my body. It was wet, but I didn't fucking care. I had to hide, had to hope that its stench kept it from being able to smell me.

Just as I was ducked in, covering myself with moss, I heard the footfalls. They were pounding along the ground, and I could feel them getting closer. God, I wanted to scream, wanted to shriek to my parents that they were right, that I was stupid, and that I should never have come looking for what killed them.

"Fuck," I heard a male voice say, and I held my breath, praying that it wasn't the beast, but knowing it had to be.

He'd stopped, standing close to where I was, and he

was looking around.

"Think, Brax," he said, then his eyes looked right at the spot I was.

I could see him, but I didn't think he could see me.

"We have to go," he said, reaching his hand down to me.

I didn't move, hoping he'd not seen me.

"I'm not the monster," he said. "Trust me. I saw you, saw you run, and I came to save you. If you don't believe me, then when we get back to our cars, you can fuck off to wherever it is you came from. But please, don't let me have to watch my vision come true."

Chapter 14

Braxton

but please, don't let me have to watch my vision come true," I begged.

It took a moment, but then she squeezed herself out from under the log she'd been hiding in. Taking my hand, she froze. Her eyes went wide, and I knew she saw what I had seen in the hut. She saw what had been planned for her. She also saw that I was honest, and was not the monster she thought was chasing her.

"Come on," I said, pulling her up to her feet.

I took her around the way, running in an arc around where I knew the clearing was. I could hear noises coming from that direction, and tried not to think about what Liwen was going through. I had to hope that he could either kill it or escape it once we were clear of the area.

Forever and a day we worked our way toward the main road that had our cars. I hoped they were strong enough to keep the beast out of them, but I wasn't sure. I knew we had to get out of there, and I'd given Liwen my keys. I was parked behind her car, so if we were gonna get out of there, we were gonna have to move my truck off to the side to get hers around it.

Chapter 15

Harper

I trusted him. I didn't know why, but I knew he was there to save me. I had to follow him, had to believe that he was my hero, my savior, the one who would keep me safe.

The screams from behind us were so loud I had to cover my ears to block them out. They hurt my everything, booming inside me, even as I had my ears covered. I stopped in my tracks, falling to the ground, writhing in pain. I felt the tearing of flesh, the ripping of muscle, the breaking of bones. Everything was within me, and I didn't understand why.

Chapter 16

Braxton

Two weeks later…

"You're sure?" I asked her.

"Yeah," she said.

"Because we can cancel if you're not up for it," I said.

"We have to go," she said. "We have to honor him for what he did for me."

"They would understand," I said.

"Shut up," she said. "We're going. To honor him. To remember what he did for me, for us."

"Okay," I said, opening the door to my truck.

The drive to the reservation was long, but we rode in silence. When we pulled up, they were all gathered. Liwen was wrapped and on his tower, ready to be released back to the earth he'd come from. Ashes to ash, and dust to dust. We would say goodbye, and then he would be returned to the ground he found so sacred, so pure, so perfect. He would be free, just as we were. He'd slain the giant, killed the beast, and freed us all.

Epilogue

Harper

One year later…

Two years ago, my parents died at the hands of a beast. One year ago, I nearly faced a similar fate. Instead, a hero slayed the beast, and an honorable man rescued me. Now, we're a family and a growing one at that. Today we went back to the site, during the day, to honor both my parents and a man I never met, paying homage to the sacrifices they gave.

Mild Corruption
Sami Ridge

White through the branches.
White behind his eyes.
The last word he remembered clearly—lunacy.

Since Pam had left in search of help, he'd returned to the barn more and more for these moments, his monthly transgressions. The smells, the cold, the closeness to soil made it much more comfortable than having to experience the changes inside the house.

He dipped his head towards the moon, his nose cold with snot. This doesn't happen in a cinematic montage of two whole minutes. No, this could go on for several hours; defiant of day and enduring as birth. It was quite convenient that he had no life.

He looked to the stacked slabs of ruby beef, and up to his horses' padlocked stables. No more mistakes.

His dog he'd sent away. His family thinks he's backpacking overseas. His wife had fled.

And him? He had his solution. Blurred moon, clear head.

It started with a few mistaken passersby—the first as he stepped out of a donut shop. The woman, glaring under rule of the sun, held herself to his passing face for a moment longer than his nerves could accept. He made a small coughing noise, a *"you're weird"* to place himself above her.

But even as that left him, and the city streets of Wallingford brought him back to a place of used bookstores, small cafes, and rare sunshine, he knew that her scrutiny wasn't the last he'd have today.

He stepped onto the street, the pleasure of its Sunday emptiness giving him stride. He would go to Green Lake, have his remaining wedge of fried bread, think about how great life was. He'd catch the 62—it was beautiful to walk, but even better to be carried. And he'd listen to something folky and bordering on Christian joy—perhaps The Mamas and the Papas.

John Phillips. What a guy.

But before the tune could swing into that resounding, rich titular word, Pleasant Monday, he felt a sharp prodding from the front seats. A homeless man was playing stare tag with him. This sort of thing was less common in this part of town, even for public transit, and if not for the squinting swine from earlier, he would've happily dissuaded it in favor of his Papas.

But eight times was indeed the limit. He popped an earbud out.

"Can I help you, friend?"

The miscreant held his gaze full tilt, no breaks. He'd achieved his attention.

But Stan gave him a smile, holding the bud close to his ear. This did not change the urchin.

"Peace be with you," Stan chirped, extending his fingers in a farewell wave. He added a small nod for a last dash of defensive sweetness. The homeless man hitched his breath as if dissatisfied with his inner query, and shook his head in brisk, impatient dismissal. He looked away.

Stan's brow furrowed, a pang of wounded uselessness. The same look as Dad. The backyard. Weeds.

Oh, the park was lovely. A shock of gold blessed the lawn, urged the backs of the running children. Kites and boat sails and bubbles adorned the air, floating in a gay assembly of true American community. He couldn't help but beam. He shoved the spongy piece of donut into his mouth.

But even as he progressed into the heart of the park, his physicality seemed to prepare itself for more scrutiny. *Judgement*, almost, the predator of a religious man. He feared running into someone he knew, feared that same blow to his composure, with the added touch of their intimacy.

He stopped to study himself. They seemed only to zero in on his face. Cutting with rude audacity. No, no. No violent words. *I will not be moved.* So, he pulled out his phone, summoning its camera despite the sun's glare and the screen's imperfections. Upon seeing himself, the man who was so often mistaken for Colin Firth, he saw only what he wanted; what he knew to be true.

An honest, God-fearing man. What use to deny that?

He raised the phone above his head; this always produced the best selfie. He'd learned this on the internet, how the below angle was typical of "down bad pedophiles." Twitter was an amusing, delightful invention.

It wasn't until he'd reached the highest point, all but one chin eliminated, that he saw the cat at his ankle. Of course, he hastily turned the screen off.

It sat perfectly at his side, an average tabby wearing a little green harness. Uninterested in him, but intent on their direction, as if keeping watch for strangers. Stan crouched to his knees, aligning his sight with that of the cats. Its posture was insanely rigid. But at least it wasn't staring at *him.* So, Stan sat, expecting a young millennial to bound forward to claim it.

Their vicinity was strangely still, all the life that had greeted him suddenly pushed back towards the water. Without pre-thought, Stan said, "Come here often?" Again, he added a bobbing dance to his head- such a dandy.

A gravelly voice responded quickly, as if anxious to have been spoken to. "Something new she's trying. Tedious. But I'm glad that she did."

Their exchange was seamless. He found himself drifting with discourse. "Do you know why I'm so curious today?"

The cat waved its tail in a sea-like motion. He seemed

to be hesitating.

"It's been so odd," Stan continued. "And *invasive*. I've never felt such a spotlight on me before." He looked down. "Not since I was a boy, I think."

The cat ignored Stans invitation into his history. His next words were measured, more assured than any human. "I do. But I think it's too far from your scope to explain. We're talking, but I *am* still an animal."

"I believe in lots of things. Mostly good things, but there's a wicked thing or two to life."

The cat barked a hoarse laugh, single and loud. Stan jolted. "Please," it said. "Please put away your jolly folly. I think its interesting, a creature like yourself entertaining such a confused system of thought."

Now Stan bristled. Was he about to undergo the sort of skirmishes like the thousand he'd fallen into on Twitter? Was this cat another lost, argumentative soul?

"The path to Christ—" Stan began.

"Is a fenced dam with leaking water. Your finger in it makes it no less dangerous." A pause. "You want to know why you're suddenly so interesting?"

Stan's only option, it seemed, was truth. He had no pride. "Yes."

"Above your head—no, don't look—forms a dreadful cloud, not dissimilar to the color of my litter droppings. Your people cannot see it, but they do sense it, and that, paired with your frightfully open countenance causes pause. You've picked a curious time and place to become evil."

Now Stan barked his laugh. "I devote myself *daily* to the practice of *anti-evil.*" Yes, he knew that wasn't a thing. At least...

"Oh, sure. Alright then. Perhaps your vest shirt has caught the light just right, or your shoes are shining just so. Too true." The cat soured. "*No.* No sir, you're becoming *evil.* Disney evil, Starbucks evil... *Chick-Fil-A* evil."

Stan looked at him. He wondered about that. But the commercial was so inclusive, the French bulldog so sweet and happy, though he knew she couldn't eat their chicken. It couldn't be. "What will happen to me as this cloud takes form?"

At that moment, the talking cat sagged into a dull countenance, looking about him very much as a harnessed animal in search of answers. He turned to leave; his back legs dipped with caution.

Stan watched him, wholly changed.

In time, he met a woman. They joined lives beautifully, every morning a merging of crossed ankles and crossword puzzles. Each day she looked at him like a miracle, and he would wink and look above his head to gesture his delight.

One night, however, Stan crawled into bed, and asked her, "Why do you love me?"

She looked at him glassily, dreamily, more ready than he knew. "You're perfect."

"Am I really? Is there no part of you that's ever.... I don't know... felt repelled by anything I've ever done?"

"No," she answered unblinkingly. Sometimes he wondered if she was secretly stoned.

"You've never noticed that people move away from us on the bus? Or stand so far in line?"

"I only see you, dearest." God, but she was starting to creep him out.

"I think I might be evil, Pam."

She laughed softly. "How sexy." That was *not* a word for her.

"I think…" Stan looked around, let out a small sigh, and slapped both sides of him. "Okay. Okay. I…. have hair now… where I didn't."

Pam arched an eyebrow.

"I grow agitated when I shouldn't."

She grinned. *Leered.*

"And nearly every night, for as long as I've known you, I've been facing the strange suspicion that I do indeed enjoy taking life, whatever I can snuff out. I go out into the woods, sit for a time, and clench my back until eventually I feel as I did when I used to play 'tug' with my childhood dog. Beefie, do you remember? Of course you do, you love me. I'm so perfect, aren't I? I'm so perfectly archivable, aren't I?"

She had not, stopped, fucking, grinning.

"Would you love that I think of animals only to destroy them? That I am one, and that as clear as day I know that I'll resemble one very soon?"

She was beginning to undress.

"Pam, I killed your cat."

She paused.

"I killed your cat, Pam."

Silence.

"I put the kibosh on your Kitty Mew-Mew. He's gone. And he was delicious. Good god. I didn't even know that about cats. Did you? What am I saying? Will you help me? Because I do want help. I do—"

And like that, she was gone.

He barred himself in. He surveyed the hay, the soil, the meat, and water bowl. He felt the moon.

There was no one nearby, thankfully.

Stan crossed to the tape player. He started to speak, until the speech became a rage. In it, he detailed everything, from the night following his encounter with the talking cat, to his surrender to public scrutiny, to his increasingly indulgent habits.

He juxtaposed his time with Pam, lovely and wholesome, their adopting a pet to cement their bond... to everything that lurked beneath.

He realized that this sort of thing happens. We don't choose which haircut frames our face best, which tv program we like most, or where on morality's table we fall. He also realized that none of it made sense. He was undeniably upstanding before this moment. He'd enjoyed simple pleasures, hadn't he? Why did his name come up in the Evil lottery? Was it simply Attraction's law that he, with his collection of wool sweater vests, Super Scrabble boards, and

Parade subscriptions, should be little more than a PNW cliché? Is he what the Netflix documentaries cover so constantly?

He then acknowledged that he had a prisoner with him, in the barn. He could only manage a hamster; a small Syrian, purchased quickly and contained by a PCC bag. He nearly named him, wanted to badly, but remembered that Evil can't be bothered.

He should've watched more evil films. Anyway.

Stan advanced on his captive. He concluded to the tape that yes, the cat from that spring was right. This was his destiny.

He howled.

June

Deep Dive
Maxwell DiMarco

It's still not too late to back out, Nicki. We have extraction choppers on standby for this exact reason."

"I—I…." Visibly cringing from the effort, Nicki forced her eyes away from James and back to the capsule-shaped submersible's live camera feed, angled downwards from the sub's lower half. The young woman swallowed heavily, sweat pooling on her face as she watched the water churn beneath her. Even the slightest bobbing of the Galac-Ship invoked terror that the crane's grip on her submersible would suddenly give out, dropping her into the depths below.

"As I said earlier, Nicki, we won't force you to do this. Whether or not you join us on the dive is entirely your choice," James reiterated, the middle-aged man's calm, slightly British-accented voice skipping in and out over the split-screen video call. "That you rode a boat out onto the ocean is already a huge step to take."

"I—I know…." Once more taking considerable effort

to tear her eyes off of the water, Nicki reached up to wipe the sweat from her brow. *But... if I choose to stay, I could do so much more.*

Clearing her mind to the best of her ability, Nicki slowly closed her eyes; took a long breath through her nose, taking in the scent of the Atlantic three stories below her— *don't think about it don't think about it*—before exhaling through her mouth. "No. Thank you, James, but it doesn't matter if I'm scared—I'm not backing out now. I'm coming with you all—that's my final answer."

"*Speaking* of scared..." The sound of wet, raucous chewing resumed as a pale, slightly-sunburned man known online as "The Lord Galactic" unmuted his microphone, having resumed enjoying his "snack bag" during James and Nicki's conversation. "You've got me curious, James. What was that fear you mentioned having?"

"Trypophobia, sir," James replied—his tone was matter-of-fact, but Nicki noticed a brief moment of squeamishness as he addressed his higher-up. "It's the fear of clusters of holes."

"Hey now, James—said it before, I'll say it again, just 'Daniel' is fine with me! We're both running the same show here!" Galactic gave a radiant smile, reaching into the bag and grunting as he tore off another small handful of grapes from the larger bunch. "And no, not that one—pretty sure *everyone* knows that one. You see those videos of arms covered in puncture holes? Eeeugh! No, I meant the one you *just* mentioned."

"I just mentioned Trypophobia," James deadpanned, the assistant's familiar snark prompting a small giggle from Nicki, as well as several of the other divers on the call.

"Nice one, wiseguy, but you know what I meant." Galactic smirked, tossing his famous snack of choice into his mouth as he elaborated, "The other one: Frutophobia! I've never heard of that."

"*Fructophobia*," James corrected. He sighed; this time, Nicki could clearly discern his discomfort. "It's the fear of fruit, and the sugars—or fructose—they contain."

Pffft! Galactic let out a stifled guffaw, sending juice and bits of purple skin tumbling into his strawberry-blonde beard. James flinched away from the video feed, his higher-up expectantly staring him down with a dead ringer for the slackjawed, wide-eyed grin featured in so many of his YouTube thumbnails. A few seconds passed, the streamer's face frozen, as he seemingly waited for James to continue... his most recent assistant merely furrowed his eyebrows in response, prompting Daniel's smile to droop.

"Noooo, no no, come *ooon*, you're pulling my leg, right?" Galactic riffed, shaking his head like he'd just been told an outlandish joke. "No, you're freakin' kidding me— and I'm *just* hearing about this? James... *Alton*, my man! *How long have you been working on the show now?*"

"A month," the darker-skinned man stated flatly. His professional tone was laced with obvious disquiet. "I'm sorry, sir— *Daniel*. But *please*, wipe off your beard."

"Sheesh, James, buddy..." Galactic blinked dully, his

smile fading entirely as he pulled up his sleeve, wiping off his mouth and facial hair with a subdued, awkward snort. "I just gotta say it, maybe you could recommend Cam 12 to your doctor after this? Because no offense, but between the two of you, *she's* the one who's got balls!" While the other ten feeds were muted, the streamer's comment provoked a few visual chortles from the remaining ten submarine pilots, including a particularly raucous belly laugh from one of the older men.

"Ha… y-yeah, okay…" Nicki, for her part, could only manage a pity laugh, subconsciously shifting her legs as she awkwardly glanced aside. Noticing her unease, Galactic quickly turned back to her feed.

"Ah, hey… I'm sorry, babe, you know I don't mean any of this," Galactic apologized, absent-mindledly grabbing another grape and articulating with it as he continued. "You get me—I joke around, cross the line a bit, it's what I do. Content and all that. If it really bothers you, I can leave you out of it once we go live."

"N-no, I'm sorry, it's just—" Nicki flinched slightly as she looked over at her favorite content creator, still feeling uncomfortable. "Hey, um, do you mind just calling me Nicki?"

"Eh? Uh, sure?" Galactic piped up, words slightly slurred as he chewed through his favorite fruit. "Sorry, babe, what did I call you?"

"Well, er… besides 'Sub 12,' you've been calling me… 'babe.' Since we first spoke, actually… and you're… still kind of doing it."

"Ah, sheesh, sorry, ba—" Galactic caught himself, pausing to swallow. "Yeah, really sorry, I know you're a guest and a fan first and foremost. Just a force of habit when I talk with cute women. Sure you get what I mean, right?"

"Ha, I... sure, I guess," Nicki managed, but her laugh was genuine, her cheeks flushing slightly. "And, uh, th-thank you, by the way... that means more than you know, to hear that from you."

"Aw, no problem, and I do mean it. That's totally my bad, don't mean to come off as creepy. Thought you were sending some signals when you mentioned your age. Oh sheesh, sorry, you *are* nineteen, right? I remember you said that, so..."

Nicki's eyes widened. "Uh, yeah, don't worry, I am! I—I wouldn't lie about that—"

"*Okay,* because *that* would have been a whole other can of worms! Ha, god, can you imagine? Cancel culture would have had me *crucified!*" Galactic made a high-pitched whistle, miming wiping a hand across his brow. "Alright, but all that aside, I've got so many names of fans running through my head, I get 'em all mixed up. What's your name, again?"

Nicki blinked. "I-I... I just said—"

"*Nicki,* right! Ha, those pre-stream jitters acting up!" Galactic chuckled, setting aside his bag of fruit. "Guess it's only natural for something this big, but glad we can get all my worst fumbles sorted out before we go live—probably wishing you could go back to before you knew how awkward I am off-camera, huh?"

"Ha, n-nah... it's fun seeing the off-stream side of you." Nicki smiled meekly, glancing aside nervously. "Sorry, it's not really a big deal, I just—"

"But *hey*, Nicks? Before we do go live in a moment, I just need to give you all a heads up," Galactic interrupted, before turning to address the other cameras. "Once we get the initial introductions out of the way, I'll be calling everyone *solely* by sub number. So that's Sub 1 for me, Sub 9 for James, Sub 12 for this lovely lady here—it's nothing personal, but for the editors' sake, we'll be handling this dive military style."

James cocked an eyebrow. "That's not—"

"*Speaking* of which..." Nicki jumped as a fourth voice cut the other man off, a chestnut-haired woman closer to Galactic's age suddenly unmuting her feed. "I have friends waiting back home for us to go live, so *maybe* get started on that?"

Galactic gave an exaggerated roll of his eyes, putting on an equally exaggerated smile. "Oh I would *love* to, Jane! But maybe you noticed that one of my fans was on the verge of a *panic attack?*"

"*Still* can't be bothered to use her real name, can you?" Jane rolled her eyes in turn, letting out a scoff. "Either way, you could have gone over your stream settings while James was talking with her, instead of scarfing down those *grapes* you love to gargle so much."

"Alright, you've made your damn point! But mental health comes before streamer wealth, sis! I've always said that!" Galactic turned to his submarine's secondary monitor and began going over settings Nicki couldn't see from his splitscreen's vantage point. "Sheesh—*women,* am I right, Nicks?" Galactic commented, looking back towards the video chat with a smarmy grin.

Nicki managed another weak laugh, James shaking his head with a sigh. For her part, Nicki's attention was torn between Galactic and Jane—the other woman seemed to be glaring at her as much as she was at her brother. "S-so... 'sis,' huh? I didn't know the Galacti-Bro had a 'Galacti-Sis....'" Nicki prompted, trying to lift the tension.

"Good," Jane grunted. Leaning off-camera, she smacked a button on her sub's control panel, cutting off her audio.

Nicki let out a quiet, "Oh," at this, feeling a bit taken-aback.

"Yeah... sorry, Nicks, there's kind of a reason I don't feature her too much," Galactic admitted nonchalantly, now focused on adjusting his stream settings. "*But,* she's family, and she's just a bit of a total ocean fanatic, so might as well take the chance for lil' bro to give his grumpy big sis a special birthday gift, right? I *am* all about giving back to the world, after all... and last I checked, she's part of it."

"Oh, that's sweet of you." Nicki smiled, hesitantly looking away from Jane as the woman spitefully rolled her eyes. "Um... sorry she's acting this way... I'd be thankful for any gift from a billionaire, let alone a sibling of mine... I mean, not that I have any, but... still."

"Well, here's an exclusive in-person Galac-tip, Nicks: Any only child should count himself blessed." Galactic let out a gruff chuckle. "Turns out, money really can't buy you love. And neither does philanthropy, as it turns out."

"Mm..." Nicki hummed. She briefly considered staying silent, but... if not now, when would she have this chance again? "Hey, while I'm here? I'm really sorry about those people in... 'Gaglactic' or, um, 'Gaylactic...' w-whatever their subreddit is called now, I know they've... remade it, a few times. But, I just wanted to say: I know you can play up your traits for the camera, but... I could never think you were a bad person. Your projects and streams are really doing good for the world."

"Hmm." Galactic cracked a half-smile at Nicki's words, furrowing his brow as he navigated to his Twitch page. "Well, like I said: Some people can't be won over, no matter what you do. But, hey! Maybe the secret will be gov—"

"Hey, no though, she's right, Daniel!" One of the other pilots suddenly chimed in, their bold voice making Nicki flinch as it bounced off the metal walls of her own sub. "I should have said this back during your last update video— we *all* should have! You're a great guy! You don't need to pander to some dumbass 4chan lurkers or whatever—all the people that matter know the *real* you, and we're on your side to the end!"

"Aha, aaalright!' Daniel coughed, discretely nodding towards James' screen before glancing over at Sub 10's pilot. "Well, it's good to hear your mic is working, miss…"

"Charlie! And, oh, actually—crap, sorry, I should have mentioned when we first talked: I'm actually non-binary," the pilot corrected awkwardly, rubbing a hand through their hair. "But don't worry, Daniel, we're cool! Not offended or anything, lot of people say I don't 'present' that way. But now you know, and—"

"*Attention, all Subs!*" Nicki jumped for the third time that day as James bombastically addressed the full submersible fleet; the second time he'd done so, after pausing to help Nicki. "Lord Galactic's stream goes live in exactly two minutes! We are currently synching the Galacti-Subs' onboard cameras to the signal amplifiers within the Galac-Ship and cycling choppers; before then, are there any other concerns?"

There was a brief lull of silence; Nicki tried not to look back at the water in the meantime. After a few more moments, James dutifully added in, "To unmute your microphone, gently press the red button next to your submarine's video feed again." Nicki quietly giggled, shaking her head… it was still so surreal hearing James speak without his "ringside drill sergeant" presenter cadence.

"I *think* we're good." The pilot of Sub 11—a rather handsome caucasian man—briefly unmuted on the others' behalf, and Nicki once more mentally kicked herself for not working up the courage to get his name back on the Galac-Ship. She really hoped her breakdown hadn't ruined any chance she had with him.

"*O-kaaaay*, we're down to a minute thirty! And thank you, Scott," Galactic announced, before nodding at the other man—*Scott, that was his name.* Nicki made a mental note of it for later. "Now! James, if you don't mind, give everyone *one* final reminder of how we'll be doing this, just before we go live. I'll briefly summarize it again for the viewers at home— but for real now, if *anyone* wants to leave, then *this* really is your *last* chance. And I mean that for real this time: If you're not up for this, let the crew help you out of your sub, so we can cut your feed. Nobody wants to watch footage of an empty metal pill dangling from a crane, right?"

Several of the pilots laughed, and this time, Nicki joined in. Even so, she gave a thumbs up, just to reassure everyone she was good to go; James gave her a supportive nod before once more taking his boss's place in addressing the twelve pilots.

"To minimize confusion for at-home viewers, pilots will refer to one another exclusively via Cam Numbers. Each of the Galacti-Subs' video feeds are labeled with the submersible's respective number. You can find your own number printed on the wall just above your chair." Several of the pilots did a once over of their submersibles on James' prompting—Nicki also followed suit, as James continued, "You will *pilot* your submarine using the provided wireless controller. It is located within the alcove to the left of your chair. Per the Lord Galactic's usual stream regulations, all relevant controls have been accordingly labeled with concise descriptions of their functions."

"And *no*, just beating Galacti-chat to the punch: We're not sponsored by Logitech," Daniel cut back in. "As *always*, these are custom made, easy-to-use Galacti-motes—and I'm not putting my name on something that'll put people at risk! *One minute left, folks!*"

As Daniel butted in, Nicki suddenly realized she actually *hadn't* taken her remote—had James even had a moment to mention it before they'd noticed how she'd been acting? She nearly smacked herself upside the head, before remembering her pilotsphere was being broadcast to eleven other people—people that her panic attack likely wasted time they could have used to memorize their subs' controls.

Nicki silently kicked herself as she reached up to a small, square box indented into the left side of the pilot sphere, stationed right besides the submersible's depth meter. Just inside the box was a gaming-style Galacti-mote- the very same model Galactic used for all his videos' custom gadgets—which Nicki gave a forceful yank, grunting with agitation as she dislodged it from the molded-alcove it had been placed in. As James had said, the controls were labeled with small strips of tape reading off their respective functions: The red button to brake; the green button to accelerate; the upper right trigger to toggle thrusters, and the twin joysticks to respectively control the submersible's tilt and horizontal angle. The left joystick even had a specific amendment beneath it: "Tilt Galacti-Sub upwards 90 degrees at 29,600 feet."

Just like that, Nicki's heart was sent racing all over again. Her eyes locked on that otherwise insignificant label, her breathing quickening. *Damn it, what was I thinking agreeing to this? Why would I ever think this was a good idea for me?*

But, no sooner had those thoughts returned to her mind, Nicki felt bad for thinking them. Tensely setting her jaw, she answered her own question. *Because anyone else would have killed to be in my position, that's why.* She sighed to herself as she secured her grip on her remote—right thumb over the green and red buttons, left thumb over the joystick—just like Galactic in his highlights. *What other girl would have the chance to conquer her biggest fear alongside her favorite streamer, and be paid to do it? This could change my life, and I'm crying like a child at the dentist.*

No. This would *not* defeat her. James' final directions faded into the back of Nicki's mind. Everything did—from the sweat forming on her palms, to the rocking of the Galac-ship, as she closed her eyes.

A deep breath. Eight seconds in through the nose... eight seconds out through the mouth.

This time, Nicki didn't need to force herself—when her eyes opened, she was already looking towards the submarine's exterior video feed. Her racing heart slowed—if only the tiniest bit—as she murmured to herself, maintaining eye contact with the looming beast that was the ocean waves.

"You won't defeat me today. This one's for Daniel... and for my new li—"

And then the stream went live.

"*Hell-o*, Galacti-chat! Wave those rainbow flags, spam your trans rights hashtags, and let's all have a *gay* old time—I'm the Lord Galactic, and *welcome* to the *first stream* of the Lord Galactic's *Pride Month!*"

The cameras were rolling, and Daniel took center stage. Smile stretched so wide his molars were on display, the one and only Lord Galactic watched with overflowing energy as the comments poured in. "And before we get started, I'd like to give a quick shoutout to..." With a faux-grunt of exertion, Galactic hoisted up a bright pink tee-shirt, proudly branded with a rainbow-filtered caricature of his most iconic expression. "...my good folks over at *Galactees*, who've once again whipped up an *incredible* Pride Shirt that somehow made my face even *more* fabulous! So pop on over after the stream and use the 24 hour codeword 'spacerainbow' to get forty-percent off, with fifty-percent of all proceeds going to verified LGBTQ+ charities! This is the kind of shirt that turns guy-friends gay and dyke-friends bi— check the pinned comments on Twitch and YouTube for this month's Charity of Choice, and let's help bring a little color back into this whitewashed world!"

Dropping the shirt on the floor of the sub, Galactic

pulled his snack bag back onto his lap in its place, snatching a handful of fruit from the bursting plastic storage unit. "Aah, I see you there, Black_Snow! Knew one of you in chat were going to mention Logitech—plain and simple, the answer's no. Now *here's* what's *really* going down, chat: Exactly *one month ago,* I have *paid off* the United States government to allow me *exclusive, premiere* diving access to the Marianas Trench, following a *record-breaking* tectonic shift at *precisely* twenty-nine *thousand,* six-*hundred* feet down! That's deeper than Everest's tall, halfway to the bottom of Challenger's Deep, and today, *you're* getting a front row seat, to accompany me into the dangers of the depths! *Will* this become the start of *Atlantic* Rim?! Will Galactic Productions be rolling out our first *combat mechas* by the stream's end?! There's only one place to find out, and today, me, James and ten other lucky recruits are going to do just that, right *here...* right *below us!"*

So his introductions are *unscripted....* So star struck by the streamer's apparent improvisation, Nicki had to do a double take before she realized that *she* was being displayed on the stream's playback monitor, the camera in her submarine that had only been used for her facecam prior now glowing with a green light. She quickly tried to put on a smile, but by the time she spiked the lens the light had already gone out, the camera back to Galactic.

"Ay, GranolaToad24, thank you for the bits my man! Now, I *know* you already know me, and you might know James if you've seen the *awesome* behind-the-scenes vlogs he's been sharing—he ain't married yet, by the way, for all you manly hunks out there. But did you know that not *one*, but *several* of my co-pilots on this expedition are chat members just like you?" Galactic challenged the camera, popping a grape into his mouth. "It's true, and *you* can join me on my next stream if you enter our weekly Galactic Sweepstakes, plus win any sort of *exclusive* cash prizes, as listed on our official website, linked in my channel description! So alright, everyone, you know the drill: Tell everyone at home why you're here, and be sure to throw in your names so they can ask for your autograph after our next *Galactic Expedition!*"

There was a moment of silence, Nicki feeling like she was going to burst from happiness—only for that ecstatic joy to be replaced with mild confusion, when an elderly woman's voice came over the video chat.

"Well, hello, everyone... I'm Ellen Rivera," the gray-haired pilot of Sub 8 spoke up, her voice somewhat shaky, and her words drawn out. "I am the owner of Delores' Daffodils, in Asheboro, North Carolina. Business has become slow lately, but this kind young man's company has offered to put eighty thousand dollars into my mortgage, if—"

"*Thank* you, Mrs. Rivera, but first names only, please!" Galactic promptly cut in, his smile looking slightly strained. "And besides, I was mainly talking to our three lucky winners, who'll be providing you coverage from Subs ten through twelve! Two lovely ladies and a gentleman, here to conquer the ocean's deep! And don't leave us with dead air, you three—*brag* a little bit! As the one and only Galacti-Bro, I decree that you've earned it! Scott, let's start with you!"

"Uh, yeah, hey—I'm Scott," Scott spoke up from Sub 10, and Nicki's face promptly went red upon hearing his baritone voice—she *really* hoped the camera wouldn't switch back to her prior to her introduction. "Know none of us like a guest who holds up the stream, so I'll just say I've been a fan of the stream since... sheesh... maybe around 2019? *Long* time now. But, long story short, good to be here... and, hey, maybe now Reddit can stop clowning that only stupid kids and ugly guys can get onto this stream."

God, you can say that last part again. Nicki couldn't hide her awkward smile—for anyone else, she'd be skeptical as to why they wore a full pressed suit on a submarine dive... but goddamn, Scott made it work. Barely even hearing Charlie as they started introducing themselves to the stream, Nicki silently made a vow to herself. *You are getting his number by the end of this.*

"...so yeah, ever since, I've been the *biggest* stream regular! I'm *absolutely* a stan, I admit—though I *swear* I'm not literal stalker-level creepy!" Charlie blathered on, apparently disagreeing with Scott's stance on prolonged introductions. "But even then, I had no fuckin' idea I'd *ever* wind up winning the Sweepstakes for something *this* big! So I just want to let the editors know: I give you full permission to mute me if need-be, because I *will* be fan-squeeing ninety-five percent of the time Daniel talks! Let's *goooo!*" Charlie did an ecstatic shimmy, letting out one such squee, before quickly looking back to the camera, "Oh, right, and it's totally chill that Daniel slipped up again, but just for the record, I'm—"

"And let's move onto *this* lovely lady, our final winner of the week!" Daniel butted in, Nicki's heart skipping a beat as her camera turned on. "And in fact, I'd like to give her a little extra time here, because she has a pretty powerful statement for you all! Care to share with the world?"

"Um… u-uh…" Nicki's heart sank as she felt her throat seize up. *Crap, shoot—shit! No, keep it together!* "U-um… I-I'm… my name's Nicki, and… s-sorry, but… I don't know what—"

Fortunately for her, Galactic quickly stepped in. "*Nicki here is doing way more than just helping out for my latest stream:* Not only is she *rocking* that fearless transgender representation—let me see those flags, people—she's actually *thalassophobic!* That's the fear of deep water, for anybody who somehow doesn't know—and I don't know about you, chatters, but I think that's pretty *damn brave!* So this week's Galac-tip is dedicated to the Phobia Slayer: Don't be afraid to face your fears head-on, because you'll *always* have friends there to support you!"

"I-I…" Nicki wasn't sure whether to feel embarrassed, terrified, or the happiest she'd ever been. "…th-th-thank you… th-thank you, so much….." Though, she had to admit, 'Phobia Slayer' did have a good ring to it.

"But enough stalling! I know what you're all here

for—I mean, *besides* me!" Galactic threw the camera a knowing wink, before raising a fist in determination. "You're here to hear James' iconic voice, kicking things off! So fire up the cranes, people, because today, we're going on our most literal deep dive yet: Twenty-six *thousand leagues* under the sea!"

With a roar of machinery, Nicki felt her submarine shake as her crane shuddered to life above her, and began lowering her alongside the rest of the twelve-person fleet into the waiting depths. She heard Charlie let out an enthusiastic "Oooooh shit—" over the video call, proceeded moments later by James' booming countdown:

"Five! Four! Three! Two! One—Operation Deep Dive is a *go!*"

And then there was an abrupt *clang* as the subs' cranes disconnected, leaving the Galacti-Subs to sink into the Atlantic.

Her heart had been racing nonstop, yet now, Nicki couldn't tell if it was still beating. The safety net of the waves had given way—she was falling. Nicki could watch it happening. She *had* to watch it happen, as her submersible's only exterior camera bore ever downwards into the looming depths of the sea, displaying a vision lifted straight from her worst nightmares.

Those unknowable depths that had chilled her to her very core, calling to her on the wind every time she looked off the side of the water shuttle back home... they had finally done good on their wordless promises, and absorbed her into the abyss. And she had no choice but to wait, and watch, as she plummeted down to meet whatever would be there to greet her.

"...primary power on, everyone! Sub 12, do you read me? You're looking a little pale there."

"H-huh?!" As if receiving a defibrillator to the chest, Nicki snapped back to the present with a jolt of adrenaline, quickly starting up her submarine's primary power with the black button in the center of the remote. As the onboard engines powered on with a rising hum, her eyes shot over towards Galactic as she spoke in a voice far closer to a shriek than she'd have preferred, "I-I'm *fine*, Sub 1, *don't worry!*"

"Copy that; just checking in." Galactic nodded, plucking a grape as he powered on his own sub with his free hand. "Everybody back home's rooting for ya—don't want to lose a good man a minute into the dive!"

"A min—" Nicki blinked dumbly. *A minute? They'd been under for a minute?!* Choking back a sob, she curled in on herself, putting her head in her hands. "I-I'm so sorry, everyone, I-I... I d-don't want to...." Nicki's voice died in her throat. Even she herself wasn't sure how she wanted to finish that sentence.

Yet this time, a voice managed to cut through her racing thoughts. "Steady breaths, dear," Sub 8's pilot reassured, Ellen's quiet voice barely audible over the video feed's white noise. "What you're doing is very brave. I can tell that the Lord is with you today."

"Yeah, second that, Nicki—we're in this thing together," Charlie added from Sub 11, their supportive smile highly noticeable within the twelve-way call as they leaned into their camera lens, as if eying Nikki through a peephole. "Keep your chin up, girl! And hey, if you need help making it down to the twilight zone, we can chat it up in the meantime! I'm sure James can filter things so we won't bug anybody else."

"The... what about the Twilight Zone?" Nicki questioned, confused by Charlie's reference as she glanced over at the screen—this only caused them to laugh as they realized Nicki's mix-up.

"*Pffft*-no, not the freakin' show—like, the Mesopelagic Zone! You know, Sunlight Zone, Twilight Zone, Midnight—you get it."

"O-oh!" Her fear briefly forgotten, now Nicki just wanted to dope-slap herself. She quickly wiped her eyes before looking back to Charlie, "Sorry, that's my bad. I really should have assumed as much....."

"Eh, no biggie, honest mistake—probably thought I was cracking wise again," Charlie shrugged, flashing a smile as they sat back in their chair, finally powering on their own submarine. "Offer stands though, Nicki! If you need somebody to take your mind off—"

"Sub 11," James interjected, his bombastic tone discarded for now. "A reminder: Please use proper pilot designations to refer to individuals."

"Oh, shoot—sorry, sorry," Charlie quickly apologized.

"But hey, Sub 8, while you're here, can you hook me and Nicki up with a more direct connection? She just looks like she could use a diving buddy, you know?"

"Of course he can! We all appreciate your concern, Sub 11, and I'm sure Sub 8 can easily give you and Sub 12 your own channel," Galactic chimed in, giving Charlie a thumbs up. "Just, *really* do try and use your Galacti-Sub numbers, alright? Again, it's not really me, it just makes things easier on the editors."

"Aaah, gotcha. Will do!" Charlie gave a thumbs up in return. "Just wanted to offer, anyway—don't mean to blab Sub 12's ear off if she doesn't want it."

"N-no, no, thank you, Sub 11. I... think I'll be okay now, but I do appreciate it," Nicki gave a small smile. "I won't let my fears hold us up any longer."

"*Speaking* of time, let's 'dive' right into our upcoming stream schedule!" Galactic prompted, face lighting up as he spiked his onboard camera. "Because you know the worst part about the old 2010 dives? They took *too long!* Hours heading down and up, plus time working out the sub schematics, time for pre-emptive therapy, or counseling, or whatever—not on my watch! We've got a *mystery* down there, and those government fat cats didn't retract their claws for cheap! That's why for the Galacti-chat's premiere deep dive into the ocean blue, I chose to expand upon our predecessors' designs to keep things moving! If everyone would just follow my lead..." Lifting his remote up for the camera, James cut himself off as he compressed the right trigger.

Nicki mimicked Galactic's action in synch with the other pilots, and jumped as the hum of her submarine's engine violently sputtered. "U-um, is it supposed to—" She began, only to be cut off by the engine suddenly peaking in volume, followed by what sounded like deafening water jets spinning to life on the Galacti-Sub's peak.

"...then everyone at home should hear the rush of our *Galacti-Subs'* newly-patented, *turbo-powered* onboard propellant system powering up, and be getting a multi-camera view of Challenger's Deep in exactly *thirty minutes!*" Galactic announced proudly, looking more than pleased with his latest technological achievement. "That's right—no waiting, no therapy, no dead air! And you can bet it took some haggling to get our team's science nerds to hook this all up before the deadline, but when the Galacti-Bro sets out to conquer a new frontier, he gets *results!* No mountain's too high, no desert's too hot, and you can bet no ocean is too deep!"

"*Woooo! You rock,* Galacti-Bro!" Charlie whooped, their enthusiasm getting a laugh from Galactic.

"Nah, nah, Sub 11, *you're* who rocks!" Galactic shot back, giving the camera a wink and a beaming smile. "You *all* rock! Because you know what? I wouldn't be here now if it weren't for all of you! That's what the Lord Galactic is really all about—giving back to the—"

"Excuse me, Sub 1? I... think I'm having technical difficulties."

Caught off-guard, Galactic's words trailed off as Scott piped up unexpectedly. "Uh... oh? Copy that, what's going on, Sco—erm, Sub 10?" Galactic stumbled, looking over to the other man's video feed. Nicki did the same, the camera showing Scott rhythmically pressing and releasing his controller's right trigger.

"So, okay: When I went to activate the thrusters, everything onboard just kind of..." Scott holds down the trigger, glancing at the camera apologetically. "...yeah, it conked out. Sorry to say, but it looks like I'm sinking at my own pace here."

Sinking. Nicki's face went pale, as Jane once more unmuted from Sub 2 over the video call, "Daniel, if these goddamn tin cans make me have to bail you out of *another* lawsuit—"

"*Copy that,* Sub 10, don't worry your head!" Galactic promptly cut off both his sister and Nicki's racing mind, giving the camera a reassuring look. "That's precisely why I had us dropped into the ocean blue right-side up; we'll get your crane down to retrieve the submersible, no sweat."

Nicki let out a huge sigh of relief, Scott giving the camera a smile and thumbs-up. "Awesome. Thanks, Sub 1." Galactic returned the smile, but raised his hands defensively.

"Hey now, you can drop the formalities, Scott— you're not on the content crew anymore! For you, Galacti-Bro will do just fine!" Galactic beamed. Pausing briefly, he cocked a brow as a thought occurred to him. "And hey, funny coincidence: With you back up at the ship, your sub can provide the dives' 'therapeutic' factor by giving us pilots a peek back at the surface! Know that I've never said it on-stream until now, but 'mental health *does* always come before streamer wealth,' after all!"

"Ha, alright, sure." Scott shrugged good-naturedly, leaning back in his chair as the sound of a lowering crane could be heard over his onboard mic. "Honestly, I'm just thrilled to be here at all, so just say the word if I can help you out, man."

"Oh come on, Scott! You're the fan—that's supposed to be my line!" Galactic laughed, before extending a mock-instructing finger. "Say 'hi' to the editing crew for me! I'll be back to micromanage their work in an hour, tops!"

Scott nodded with a friendly chuckle. "Will do, Galactic."

"I mean, I *do* prefer Galacti-Bro, but whatever my man, call me what you like! Glad to have you on the stream, Scott." As Scott's submarine was re-attached, Galactic stuck his hand back into his grape bag, looking aside as he thought to himself. With an awkward laugh, he then looked back over at the video call. "Okay, crud—help me out, folks, where was I? Sub 12? 11? Were you two girls keeping track?"

"Um…" Nicki began, scratching the back of her head. Charlie was notably silent. "Well, you and Charlie were talking, but besides that—" Leaning forward in their seat with a sigh, Charlie cut Nicki off.

"Hey, Sub 12? Actually, sorry, but can you let me handle this one?" Charlie asked; their inflection was polite, but Nicki couldn't help but notice the subdued undertones of exasperation. Nicki nodding, her concern clear, Charlie looked over to Galactic. "Okay, listen. Sub 1."

Galactic's smile wavered slightly as he looked toward Charlie—his eyes subtly danced around their own. "Is something else wrong now, Charlie? I can send—"

"Ah ha—so *now* you default to my name!" Charlie clapped their hands, a look of validation on their face. "It's exactly what ol' Fleming says; once is an accident, twice is a coincidence, but *three times*... yeah, I bet you just now caught yourself, didn't you?"

His smile strained at those words, Galactic's eyes locked with Charlie's. "I'm sorry... what? I think there's a failure to communicate here."

"You know what? Yeah, there is!" Charlie snapped, Galactic losing his smile as he flinched backwards. "I'm sorry, Daniel, I don't wanna be that fan, but I'm *not* a girl, and that's three times now you've 'slipped up—' two of them were on-camera, and for one of 'em, couldn't help but notice you cut me off before I could correct you!"

"*Whoa, hey,* what're you getting at here?" Daniel's eyes darted between Charlie and his livestream—swallowing heavily, he grabbed two more grapes and shoved the handful into his mouth before responding, "Uh... *kind* of a rough move to try and call me out while we're live, don't you think? You all know me, I've only got so much mental capacity; if this meant so much to you, you really should have mentioned it when we first—"

"'Meant so much to me?!' You didn't think my *gender* was a big deal?!" *Now*, Charlie was done, and their rising volume reflected that. "And don't give me that crap about memory! We're one guy, one girl, one agender—couldn't be simpler! How would you like it if I called *you* a woman?!"

"Y-you—rrrghffff—" Daniel sputtered wordlessly, spitting grape skin across his pilot sphere as he shoved his palms into his chest. "No, you know what, I'm tired of this immature rumor! Do I *look like I have breasts?!*"

"W-whoa, what fucking side of you is *this* now?!" Charlie gaped, now quickly becoming just as aghast as they were furious.

Nicki's eyes switched frantically between the two pilots, the tensions rising rapidly. "Okay, once and for all, let me make this clear: I am, and always have been, a *cisgendered man!*" Daniel announced loudly, more so to the livestream than to Charlie. "Everyone, I'm sorry I even had to address this—the editors will crop this out for the YouTube folks—but I'm not going to be wrongfully labeled a transves—"

"I wasn't saying you're *shit!* I'm saying *you've* been misgendering *me* the whole goddamn day!" Charlie screamed, grabbing the camera as if trying to seize Daniel himself by the face. "And I *was* just going to set the record straight, but *now?* I don't even know who I'm looking at anymore! Did all those pro-LGBTQ intros *hurt* you to read aloud?!"

"Ch-charlie, Daniel, please calm—" Nicki tried to step

in, but apparently in person Daniel wasn't content to let a fan fight his battles.

"Charlie, come on—GranolaToad, thank you for the bits, I'll get back to you in a sec—but Charlie, are you seriously going to call me out over some little mistake, and me rightfully getting upset at a constant, *demoralizing* insult?" Daniel set his jaw, his approachable front discarded as he crossed his arms. "I'm sorry, but I think I speak for the whole Galacti-chat when I say: That's pretty darn petty. I'm sure the LGBTQ+ will *love* having themselves be represented by a self-absorbed, non-binary bimbo with poorly-repressed anger issues." Daniel smirked, glancing over at his chat, which was now going by a mile a minute, "Hey-hey, sheesh, if I knew the pilots were going to act like this, maybe we *did* need the pre-dive therapy after all, am I right?"

Charlie let go of the camera, clenching their fists. "Okay, fine... I'm sorry too or whatever you want to hear, but the *least* you can do is *try* to keep these things in mind!" Daniel only shrugged at this and shook his head, clearing believing he'd won. Charlie's eyes narrowed in response. "No I mean, seriously! You clearly remember *Scott's* name just fine, don't you? What's up with that, huh?"

"I'd think that would be obvious, Charlie," Jane spoke up out of nowhere, her eyes glued on her brother; upon hearing her monotone voice, his eyes narrowed into squints, Jane scoffing at the sight. "Honestly now, did you think you were being *subtle,* Daniel? Featuring the *one* presentable adult male in your viewerbase doesn't prove anything.

You're a face for the lowest common denominator—you contribute *nothing* to society, and you never will."

All eyes now on Jane, Charlie was about to speak up, but once again, Daniel stepped in—*aggressively.* "You know what, *Jane?!* Let me say this now, so *everyone* at home can hear this, or archive it, or meme it or whatever they wind up doing: The *truth* is, I've done more for this world than you *or* my parents ever have! And if you want to snap at me the *one* time I'm trying to extend a damn olive branch, and let my nobody 'marine-biologist sister' be part of the stream that's saving third-world nations on a *daily basis,* then that's on you!"

"You've been hyping up your pointless projects since you were born, Daniel, and they're still just as irrelevant now!" Jane suddenly snapped, becoming *far* more emotive out of nowhere as both she and Daniel alike leaned into their cameras. "The only difference is that now, when you throw vehicles into pits and fill rooms with plastic balls, instead of Mom and Dad reprimanding you, the neckbeards and children who watch you are throwing unearned money into your insatiable gullet! 'Saving nations—' that's complete horseshit. Your audience doesn't care about that, and neither do you. Your 'brand' is the enabling of a constant cycle of self-aggrandizing publicity stunts, while using the world as your playground. You're just the same as you ever were, Daniel Kramer, and that's *all* you'll be remembered as!"

Daniel's eyes flashed with rage, the streamer baring

his teeth in a grimace, "Now *listen here*, you entitled little—Black_Snow, I *told you* we're not sponsored by Logitech!!"

FWOOSH

"A-ah?!" Having been watching the back and forth in stunned silence, Nicki's breath caught in her throat as a massive blur of color audibly rushed past her video feed of the surrounding water. "D-did anyone... did anyone see that?" she asked meekly, only for her voice to be lost in Jane and Daniel's squabbling.

"Sub 12?" James spoke up; also having settled into quietly watching the Kramer siblings verbally lash at one another's throats, his face was now intent, alert. "What did you see?"

"Huh? Nicki, you good?" Charlie questioned, looking over to the anxious woman's feed. "Stay with us, girl, these two clearly have some things to—"

"N-no, there's—" Nicki began. It had happened so fast! "I think I saw….."

"Holy shit—*Galactic?!*" It was Scott's voice. And though the streamer didn't notice the fearful exclamation, Nicki sure did. "Either the lens is—*nope*, there's *something* in the water by the ship! It looks like some kind of, hand, or—"

What happened next finally broke through Daniel and Jane's shouting match: The unmistakable sound of *metal* being torn into, as Scott let out a yell and cringed in on himself, his video feed thrown sideways.

"Sc-Scott?! What's going on?!" Eyes wide, Daniel scrambled into his seat, more horrible metallic squealing rising from Scott's feed. "Is something attacking the—"

FWOOSH

Daniel's voice caught in his throat, a second blur of color speeding past his own submarine's outer camera as Scott stammered in response, "I-I don't know!! I-it feels like the ship just struck something; I think that something just...."

Scott's eyes drifting to his own exterior video feed, his eyes widened in fear. "Oh my god—*oh my god, we're fucking tilting*—there's another one! There's another one *right below*—" Scott was cut off once more, as the same metal scraping rang out once more... right on top of him. The younger man let out a scream of terror as what looked like massive, bloodied *claws* pierced his submarine's walls, moments before his video cut off with a violent spark.

"*Scott!*" Nicki screamed, even knowing it was too late—her heart was sinking faster than her submersible, and they'd already begun the transition into the midnight zone. "Oh my god, oh my *god!*"

"Oh, shi—st-stay calm, everyone! Chat, hang on, we're getting out of this... *Jane!*" Daniel screamed for his sister once more, but this time he was *far* from angry. "What on earth was *that*?!"

"What are you expecting *me* to do? I'm not your fucking Pokédex!" Jane snapped back, her eyes frenzied and wild. "No, you know what, I will tell you what it is—it's an unidentified species with a carapace hard enough to puncture *steel*, and it just *killed* your entire crew! And it's highly probable you've put us into a direct course towards its *feeding ground!*"

"Lord have mercy on us all...." Ellen quietly murmured in Sub 8, before her words were overtaken by a cavalcade of the other pilots' voices, Charlie and Nicki chief among them.

"Daniel, did you know these things were down here?!" Charlie demanded, their anger quickly returning.

"O-oh my god, oh my *god*, wh-what are we going to do?!" Nicki stammered, clutching at her heart. "W-we're going to die... *we're actually going to die!*"

"*Everyone,* stay calm! No one is dying!" Daniel commanded, before realizing what he'd said. "I-I mean, besides Sco... a-heh, well, we don't know if they're *really* dea—"

"That's it! I didn't sign up for this!" a disheveled-looking man suddenly piped up from Sub 3, fiddling with his controller. "I'm done! I'm not going any deeper!"

"Sub 8!" another scraggly-looking individual spoke up from Sub 5, clearly wrestling with the Galacti-mote. "Tell me how the hell to turn this death machine around!"

"*No one is turning around!*" Daniel suddenly screamed, eyes wide as his cracking voice peaked his sub's microphone. Glancing at the chat, he took a shaky breath in. "L-listen: Galacti-bro doesn't go into these things unprepared, especially not with his *favorite* sister with him! So if everyone can stay calm, I can tell you—"

"For God's sake, nobody here is staying *anything,* you

fucking pussy!" another older man screamed from Sub 7—Nicki recognized him as the one with the particularly exaggerated laugh at Daniel's earlier tasteless joke. "Stop prancing around solutions like a spineless pansy and direct your damn fleet!"

"*Not now, Thomas!* Shut up and let me explain things, you goddamn bums!" Daniel snapped, his breath quickening by the second. "*Listen!* The stream is still broadcasting from the choppers—the folks back at Galactic HQ can send out a rescue team! But for now, whatever attacked Scott is up there, and we're down here, so our best bet is to *keep! Moving! Down!*"

"Have you lost your damn mind?!" Jane balked, slamming her fist into her pilot sphere's wall. "Is your ego so fucking swollen it's blocking out anything I say?!"

"I *know* what you said, and you're going to kill us all!" Daniel snapped back, pressing a blue button on his Galacti-mote. At the bottom of Sub 1, dual lights switched on with a sizzling of electricity. "Get your lights on, people! The threat's up there, and for better or worse, most likely occupied with the Galac-ship! If we go back up, we'll just be drawing its attention away from an ideal distraction!"

"Wh-what?! Distract—Daniel, you can't be serious!" Charlie objected, hand clenched hard on their forehead in disbelief. "As much as I hate to give your bitch of a sister the time of day, we know there's *two* already—and it doesn't take a marine biologist to presume that there's *going* to be more!"

"You see, you cocksmoking fruit?!" the Sub 7 pilot—evidently named Thomas—barked at Daniel, "Even your dyke of a sister and the fucking spik snowflake know you're full of shit!"

"*Wow*, okay! Nice slurs, you crumbly old corpse!" Charlie snarled, glaring daggers at the lighter-skinned man. "You know, I always *wondered* why Daniel would never introduce his regular volunteers, but good fucking riddance to you!"

"And good riddance to all of this retarded online programming, you job-stealing harlot!" the racially-charged bum seethed back, spittle flying into his beard. "I'd rather stay anonymous and walk away with a paycheck than be pointlessly humiliated in front of a crowd of—"

And then, Nicki screamed.

"*There's something down there!*"

This time, Nicki *saw* the creatures approaching from far below, illuminated in the wide lighting of Sub 1—but what she saw wasn't the "hand" that had taken Scott. *These were an approaching flock*—a *swarm* of twitching, grasping, almost *crustacean-like* beings, their tail-like bodies and multitude of thin, insect-like legs wiggling behind oversized heads that ended in several jutting spikes of flesh, said heads covered in countless, beady eyes. And all of them—Nicki could count at *least* twenty—were heading *right for the fleet.*

Watching the colony approach unblinking, James coldly shook his head. "We have soft contact," he murmured, looking to his own feed of the livestream as the other pilots flew into even more of a frenzy.

"Holy shit—what are those, shrimp?!"

"We need to leave, *now!*"

"Shut up! Everyone just *shut up, okay?!*" Daniel screamed in vain, even as his eyes remained locked on his own submarine's feed. "Nobody try anything. I'll just turn off my lights, we don't know if they're hostile—*Jane!*"

"Fuck you, Daniel!" Hands tight on her remote, Jane turned on her sub's exterior lights and jabbed the tilt stick forwards, her pilot sphere's framework squealing as the submersible slowly began its rotation into a horizontal position, fighting the thrusters' downward propellant. "You and the other societal rejects can dive straight into a watery grave, but I'm not depriving my field of the *actual* Kramer prodigy!"

"What did I say?! You're not going to *get* anywhere!" Daniel gawked, his face red as his heart pounded out of his chest. "I planned for all of this, you moron! Listen to me for once in your damn life, or you're going to lose it!"

"No, *you* listen to her! She's the only one in your family who's not a fucking retard!" Thomas suddenly spat, following Jane's lead, "Have your yes-men drop the eighty grand off at the shelter, you prissy little faggot! I'm leaving!"

"*What did you just call me,* you talking corpse?!" Daniel practically shrieked, eyes bugging out of his head as several more pilots followed suit in rotating away from the rapidly approaching entities. "No, stop, *stop! Turn off* your damn lights and *stop moving,* you idiots! Just *pay attention to—"*

"Turn off your boosted propellant systems!" James suddenly yelled, causing Charlie to freeze just as they were about to follow suit with the escape efforts. "The Galacti-Subs require five minutes to reach a horizontal position, ten to rotate a complete one-hundred eighty degrees; if you attempt to force a rotation at heightened acceleration, it could cause horrible structural damage!"

"Blargabladda heightened structural *damaaage...*" Thomas parroted in an unidentifiable accent, jabbing the acceleration button as a rising squeal of steel sounded from above him, "Take your ass back to England, you goddamned limey nig—"

What followed was a series of echoing *snaps*—first from Thomas's feed, and then in progressive order from Jane through each escaping submersible, as the "turbo propellers" systematically snapped off from the end of the subs. There was a moment of silence within the fleet's video call, the pilots interchangeably staring in seething disbelief at one another, or awaiting the inevitable to emerge from the impenetrable darkness around them.

"Dear Lord, please watch over us in this time of need...." The footage flickered slightly as Ellen quietly clasped her hands, the rest of her solemn prayer lost as she fell into a whisper.

"N-Nicki?" Charlie stuttered, looking over to the cowering woman in Sub 12 with an expression that was, not from lack of trying, far from reassuring, "You... you gonna be okay?" Nicki merely whimpered in response.

"Disengage power. Compress the left trigger," James directed, his breathing shockingly steady as he turned from the video call back to his primary camera feed. "Additional onboard baggage will be discarded; the pilot sphere will return to the surface in approximately one hour forty-five minutes."

Panting heavily, Daniel looked between the ten other remaining pilots. "You see what you've done? Now you're all taking the long way up, and I've lost around five minutes of highlights to a pointless screaming match."

"Daniel," Jane seethed, speaking through her teeth, "There is a non zero chance that we are *all* about to die. Tell me you are not *still* thinking about the fucking stream."

"We're *still* online, so *yes*, I *still* am!" Daniel simply scoffed, as though Jane had just asked a clearly rhetorical question. "Guess you really are a fake fan, sis—any true member of the Galacti-chat knows I've survived *way* worse than this! When it comes to exploring the galaxy, it's just part of the job description!" Looking pleased with himself, Daniel shot his secondary monitor a smarmy grin, as a strange scuttling sound began to rise around the remaining submarines.

"Wh-what is actually *wrong* with you, you freakin' sociopath?!" Charlie demanded, their eyes wide with disbelief. "You can't just go back to cracking jokes *now*—Scott is *dead!* Th-these things killed him!"

"Oh good, here's the Gender-Neutral mascot for anger issues again! Thank god, I thought we'd lost them to the ocean blue for a minute there!" Daniel bemoaned, running a hand across his forehead as the scuttling began to rise in intensity. "You can try to over-analyze and villainize me all you want, but when push comes to shove, *I* was right, and *you* signed a liability waiver! So don't blame good old Galacti-Bro for making you all freak out and jump the— *Thomas don't!*"

One moment, the disgruntled old man was pressing down the acceleration... and the next, the scuttling gave way to a bombardment of scratching and clanging from Sub 7's exterior. "Ah, shit—god *fucking damn it!*" The man's bloodshot eyes went wild as large dents began to form in the pilot sphere, water spurting inside moments before spikes of reinforced flesh punctured the submarine's hull, the footage cutting out just as the Galacti-Sub caved in on itself with a horrible mix of imploding metal and gargled screams.

"*Dive! Accelerate and dive!*" Daniel screamed, squeezing his remote so hard it nearly broke in his palms as the fleet was swarmed from all sides, his submarine plummeting into the depths.

"Daniel, you fucking cowa-*aaaurgh!*" Jane's scream fell into wordless agony as her own submarine was breached, one of the shrimp-like beings physically ramming into her from the outside as they were both crushed by the surrounding pressurized steel like a wad of paper.

"J-James!" Nicki cried out, but James didn't respond, staring straight ahead with a steely gaze as he sent his submarine plunging after his boss. Her hands shook like she was trapped in an earthquake as she watched the video feed, yet another of the submarines penetrated by the horrible creatures.

"Nicki, girl, just hit the damn button!" Charlie pleaded, finally powering up their own submarine's thrusters, "We can activate James' failsafe later! For now, we need to go!"

"I-I-I can't—" Nicki choked on her own voice as yet *another* submarine was compromised, the pilot's scream cut off as a piece of steel lodged itself into his throat. She could *hear* the creatures scuttling around her, finally ready to pull her into their domain for good. The world spun around her, she felt like she was going to pass out... and then, through the darkness, she saw it again.

FWOOSH

"Ch-Charlie! It's ba—" Nicki was cut off by a loud *clang* sounding from Charlie's video feed.

Moments later, those hellish claws burst into Sub 11, their demolishing of the Galac-ship having left viscera and tendrils visibly dangling from the phalanges. Charlie screamed in horror as the horribly-gored limb descended upon them seconds before their feed cut out for good. Nicki could *hear* the submarine crash inwards in the water beneath her, the sound mixed with a disgusting sound of the massive limb being forcefully compressed by the very waters it had seemingly called home. Her heart feeling like it was about to explode as the scuttling fell into the briefest of lulls, Nicki let out a blood-curdling scream, nearly deafening herself as she finally pressed the acceleration, plunging her vessel ever deeper into the depths below, and leaving her fellow pilots at the mercy of the ocean's displaced denizens.

The Abyss. Also known as the abyssopelagic zone... even its proper name instilled the same dread. It was the approach to the ocean floor, a place nature's unspoken laws declared that no human was ever meant to traverse.

"He-heh..."

And yet here she was. Nicki really *was* living out her dreams... her worst damn nightmares. Trapped piloting a claustrophobic, barely-mobile undersea vessel, with *something* out in the water around her.

"Heh-hehhehheheh..."

A *something* that was not deterred in any way by the steel coffin she was sealed inside and the only way to avoid it... was to dive deeper. Further down. Far away from home. Far away from what she knew as safety. Nicki was in *their* world now. The *abyss* that lurked deep beneath the surface, eager to swallow up any foolish enough to dare its depths... and today, that was Nicki Kauer.

"Hehehehehaaaaheeeheeeheeeeh-*eeeeehhh*..."

"*Daniel,* what are you—" Nicki barked, feeling ready to snap as she glared towards the video chat... only to find the man not laughing, as it had seemed, but quietly sobbing into his hands. "Oh... n-nevermind... I'm-I'm sorry, I thought you were...."

"I think that he was, dear." Nicki jumped as she finally noticed the fourth pilot: *Ellen,* the elderly woman currently slowing her submarine's acceleration to a more steady pace. "But let's not judge him for that... as incompatible as it may seem, many will force themselves to laugh in times of tragedy. It's a stress mechanism—we're trying to fool our mind into believing we're living better lives."

"I see," Nicki quietly acknowledged, looking aside as she fell silent again.

For only the second time since she'd climbed into Sub 12, Nicki allowed herself to look at the depth meter: 16,300 feet down, and rapidly counting. They were already halfway through the abyss. Evidently Daniel really wasn't kidding when he mentioned speeding things up. The wonders of modern technology... Nicki felt like she was going to puke.

"A reminder," James interjected flatly, speaking to all four remaining pilots. "At eight-thousand, eight-hundred thirty nine meters—approximately twenty-nine thousand feet, cut power to the primary thrusters. At nine-thousand meters, we'll rotate ninety-degrees to enter the newly-created fissure."

Nicki buried her face in her hands. She felt like the entire world was going crazy. "What are you *talking* about? We're not... we're not still going through with this, are we?"

"*We* are," Daniel huffed, running an arm across his eyes and sniffing as he sat upright. "In case you forgot, babe:

James and I kind of paid off some serious government bigwigs to let us take cameras down here at all. So even setting aside the Galacti-chat back home, they're expecting *something* more cohesive than 'Host' with shrimp in Atlantis by the end of this."

Nicki said nothing in response, simply nodding as she lowered her palms back to her knees. Himself reaching for another handful of grapes, Daniel looked back at Nicki, eying her with visible pity. Plucking the fruit, he opened his mouth to speak…

"Daniel, I believe you owe Nicki an apology." But Ellen beat him to it, watching the streamer with subdued expectancy. Nicki and Daniel *both* looked over to her at this, their confusion clear.

"For… what, now?" Daniel questioned, though It came out more as a shaky rasp.

"Her name is Nicki, dear. Not *babe*," Ellen corrected him, like a grandparent gently lecturing their grandchild. "I believe she made it very clear." Nicki blinked in silent surprise, sitting up slightly; she hadn't even noticed Daniel's latest slip-up.

In contrast, Daniel just narrowed his eyes, letting out a sigh as he looked back at his stream. "Look," he began flatly, shoving his snack of choice into his jaws and chewing noisily as he continued, "this might very well be my last stream. At the very least, the last before a *long* break. Any benefits I promised you are still valid, Ellen, but if you all really don't want to follow me for the last legs of this, go right ahead."

"That's ultimately not my choice to make, sir," James stated, looking notably squeamish as he fiddled with the stream settings on his own end.

"I know, James—it's mine, and that's why I'm telling you that you can leave," Daniel specified, wiping his face clean of juice and residue. "I can guarantee you'll have enough power to reach the surface if you turn back now. But whether alone or not, a captain always goes down with his ship; that holds true no matter *what* sector of the galaxy you're exploring. And, well... ha, I've come a long way, but I'm prepared to see my career end like it all began."

Nicki watched the man with a heavy heart; indeed, for maybe the first time that day, it actually felt like she might be getting a glimpse of the real man behind "the Lord Galactic." A momentary glimpse of a man with none of his typical roast comedy, social media buzzwords or toxic, fame-induced family squabbles... was *this* who "Daniel Kramer" had really been, deep down?

She looked back at the depth meter... they were 16,700 feet down now... now 16,750 down... now 16,800... 16,850....

Any moment now, Nicki expected to hear an electric engine surge, as one of the pilots began to turn their submarine back towards the safety of the surface... yet no one did. The young woman set her jaw, straightening her posture and securing her grip on the Galacti-mote one last time.

It seems they had all reached the same decision.

There had been very little conversation after they'd passed into Challenger's Deep. The most was James reading out the current depth every thousand feet, and then cuing the other three pilots to decelerate once they neared their ultimate destination. Upon decelerating to a relative stand-still, he then began providing his final instructions.

"We should now be directly parallel to the fissure," James announced, all eyes now on him for orders. His own eyes were locked to the depth meter. "Per our consistent diving angle, upon rotating ninety degrees we will be able to enter without any further adjustments. Keep the tilt stick pressed forward until five minutes have elapsed. I will personally prompt all pilots when sufficient time has passed."

"You're the boss, my man!" Daniel nodded, the four of them pushing the left joystick upwards in tandem. "I mean... normally I technically am, but under the circumstances that's *prooobably* completely irrelevant." Nicki smiled slightly at finally hearing Daniel crack another joke.

As the Galacti-subs began rotating back, lifting cameras on the bottom ever-so-slowly into a forward-facing position, Ellen looked to Nicki over the video chat. "You didn't talk much about yourself back on the surface," the older woman stated.

Nicki started slightly upon realizing she was being spoken to. "Oh, um... y-yeah, I sorry, I... guess I underestimated how badly I do with crowds," Nicki admitted, feeling a bit embarrassed in hindsight.

"You don't have to apologize, dear—it's a learned trait," Ellen reassured her, giving a patient smile. "I was simply curious what inspired you to join us on this journey."

"W-well, I didn't really *know* if I was going to be picked," Nicki clarified, her fingers cramping slightly as she held down the joystick. She quickly readjusted her hands. "But, I've been watching 'the Lord Galactic' since I was a kid, and... well... you know...."

Letting go of her submarine's controller with one hand, Nicki motioned over herself. Seeing Ellen tilt her head, seemingly confused, Nicki elaborated. "L-like he said, I'm thalassophobic... and, well, transgender. But, until now, I've technically been... 'pre-op,' if you know what that means?" To Nicki's surprise, Ellen actually nodded, her face displaying clear recognition. Feeling relieved, Nicki continued, "S-so, um... long story short, Daniel's talked about how he usually gives his volunteers eighty-grand per video... and, given this process would cost about seventy-thousand...."

Nicki trailed off, but Ellen finished her story for her— the older woman was smiling proudly. "...you decided to start your new life by conquering your biggest fear in a supportive environment."

"Yeah!" Nicki concurred, feeling like a weight had been lifted as she returned Ellen's smile. Somehow, hearing someone else say it out loud was... validating. "Yeah, exactly... I'll be honest, I—after everything that's happened today—I really thought I was being an idiot, thinking like that."

"Oh, dear, certainly not." Ellen's smile faded, but her supportive tone remained. "Often in life, we have to experience the worst of our lives before we reach what we truly desire. And you could not have known what had been living just out of sight. But despite the loss, and the grief... the Lord has carried you through to the end. And I truly believe, Nicki, it is a sign that He has given you His blessing in your new life."

"One minute," James called out, and Nicki was pulled back to the present.

She murmured, her heart sinking anew as memories of Scott and Charlie returned to her mind's eye. "I've never really been a religious girl...."

"I understand, dear... in these times, not many are. Neither were they when I was your age." Ellen hummed quietly. "Indeed, this modern age has stressed even the Lord's hand to its limits. But even so... I've lived through both the best and worst of times. And I witnessed enough assiduous people triumph against their hurdles to know: A brave girl like you has a place reserved for her in God's plan."

Despite herself, Nicki felt tears tickle at her eyes. "It's a nice..." She stopped herself, rubbing at her eyes with her free hand. "Thank you, Ellen. I... hope I can find that place, after this is all over."

"Well, hey! I'd be willing to lend a hand there!" Daniel suddenly chimed in, giving one of his thumbnail-worthy smiles. "If we get out of this, I'll pay you whatever you need! Consider it Galacti-Bro's blessing towards the life of Nicki, the Phobia Slayer!"

"Uh... th-thank you!" Nicki replied, giving the beaming man a more subdued expression of gratitude. "Though, I really don't need any more than the normal amount... just having the extra ten-thousand to spare afterwards would be incredible!"

"Naaah, come on, twist my arm a little here!" Daniel encouraged, holding out his arm with a mock cringe of exertion. "Pretty sure that you've got the whole chat in your pocket here, Nicks—sure know you got me anyway—and all this expedition's money has gotta go *somewhere!* Come on, it's Pride Month, name your price! Or at *least* give me a charity name so—"

"Sir. We're level with the fissure," James interjected, relinquishing the tilt stick. Besides his raised volume, his face was steely as Nicki, Ellen, and Daniel followed suit, the four Galacti-Subs halting in a near-perfectly level position. "We may proceed when ready."

"Oh! Uh, wow, that was fast. Alright, well, let's *go!*" Daniel clapped his hands, switching back on the submarine's main thrusters. "Get the primary acceleration back on, people! This is the home stretch; let's get our government work over and done with, and get our wonderful volunteers their well-earned *money!* Hope you're all strapped in tight,

Galacti-chat; because *we're* finally going in!"

James nodded in response, following his boss's lead; Nicki and Ellen did the same. "Per our original dive plans, sir, the onboard spotlights would ideally be active while inside the fissure, to accommodate for rough terrain or sharp angles." James briefly paused; after not receiving an answer, he looked back at the camera. "Sir? I believe this is your call."

"Ah, right." Daniel cocked a brow, considering the available options. With the pilot sphere now leaving him essentially laying on his back, he stared out at the dark waters projected by the camera, watching the vague impression that was the western wall of Challenger's Deep slowly close in through the darkness. "Heh, I'm... kind of regretting having the lab men design these things like they did...."

"*Sir,*" James bluntly urged, looking back out at the approaching fissure.

"Okay, well," Daniel began, not without some suppressed irritation, "we haven't seen-or heard-those shrimp... *things,* in a while. I'm willing to bet this means they're still occupied out there. So I'd say... that we... are good to—"

"No."

Daniel's finger froze right over the button for the lights. "Ooof course. What have we got this time—" But as Daniel looked back at James, he found that his assistant was suddenly staring *right* at Daniel—directly at the other pilots through the camera, unblinking. "James? A-Alton?"

Silently, James motioned to the camera feed. "Listen."

So listen they did. And then, they finally heard it, over the Galacti-subs' motors: Scuttling against rock—scuttling of *countless*, swarming creatures, a din rising from the fissure they were swiftly closing the distance to... and that's when they realized *why* they could make out the fissure at all.

The western wall of Challenger's Deep was *covered* in the shrimp-like beings. Spread across the undersea crust, their razor-thin legs carried them out of the fissure in droves, their bodies outlined in tiny, luminescent lights. Some of them ran down and out of sight to the unseen sands far below, while others grouped into pairs or trios on the wall, limbs and faces snapping at unseen nutrients. It looked more like an alien *hive* than a colony of any earthly shrimp, the lights lining the creatures' torsos blinking in and out of sight as they crawled over and around one another, completely undeterred by the unprecedented undersea pressure boring down on them.

Daniel let out a pitiful laugh, eyes darting between the camera and his stream chat as sweat began pooling on his face. "Last chance to leave me to my shrimp fry, folks."

Staring out at the approaching colony, Nicki looked towards Ellen out of the corner of her eye. "Ellen... did you really do all this for your mortgage?"

"I had few other options left, dear—this was the *least* dangerous." Ellen let out a quiet laugh at that. "But, then again, at my age, you naturally start to lose your fear of the unknown. When death is always at your doorstep... I suppose I've stopped viewing him as a stranger."

Nicki's eyes turned back to the fissure. The four-sub fleet was about to cross the threshold into the colony's origin. Her eyes narrowed. "I've already gone this deep. And I've never been scared of crustaceans."

FWOOSH

It all happened in barely over a second. A rush of water rose from behind the fleet, followed just seconds later by the impact of flesh against steel, as Ellen's sub collided with something turning full-speed into the fissure from the waters beyond. Before anyone could react beyond wordless screams of shock, Sub 8 was punctured by mangled claws of skin and bone, the submersible collapsing inwards barely a second later and crushing both the attacker and the prey within an iron maiden of undersea pressure.

"You *bastard!*" Nicki screamed bloody murder as Ellen's feed went black, the remaining claw claiming its second, and *final,* human life that day. "Go to hell! I hope you *actually go to hell!*" Nicki futilely yelled at the air, as if screaming directly at the now-dead creature.

Alerted by the sound of Sub 9's imploding steel, the scuttling on the walls of the fissure increased tenfold as the massive, shrimp-like beings flew into a frenzy. Nicki watched with tears streaming down her face as streaking lights wildly flew past the exterior cameras, like a frantic swarm of undersea fireflies.

"Oh lord—this is it! This is finally it!" Daniel quaked,

his submarine buffeted as the shrimp flew between the ceiling and walls seemingly without rhyme or reason. "Everyone, watching back in the Galacti-chat! I'm going to keep the stream up as long as I can, but don't let them keep this a secret! There's *something* down here, and I'm going out right in the middle of it! This is Daniel Kramer's final message as Galacti-Bro: *Get this video out to the world!*"

FWOOSH

"There are more 'hands' coming from deeper in!" James yelled over the surrounding din, a huge shadow passing right over his submarine's camera—only now could they see that the hands were also lined with the same lights as the smaller creatures. "I repeat: The creatures that attacked the Galac-Ship are coming from *inside* the fissure, and share traits with the crustacean specimens—they appear to cohabitate!"

"*Thank you, Mr. Exposition!*" Daniel spat, knocked to the side as a particularly frenzied shrimp flew off the wall and smashed back-first into the bottom of Sub 1, its exoskeleton cracking on contact. "Chat, I swear: Archive this *now!* I don't know what those government suits will tell you, but *you* all know the truth! You can spread the word of our final voyage! Don't let the Lord Galactic's death be in—*for crying out loud Black_Snow, I'm not sponsored by—*"

FWOOSH

"H-how are there so many?!" Nicki shrieked, recoiling as yet another hand narrowly missed her own submarine. "What even *are* they?"

"I don't know, but Ms. Rivera was right: We are *absolutely* blessed that their trajectory hasn't sent them headlong into us," James replied, the nearby motion of the passing creatures audible even over the video feed. "But if they believe there's a threat *outside*, it's possible that they're evacuating their 'nest.' If this is so, our best chance for survival is—"

"James."

FWOOSH

Daniel hardly flinched as a third fleeing hand passed them by. His eyes were locked on his stream replay, watching the chat messages that were, even now, scrolling from the bottom of the screen to the top. When he spoke, Nicki couldn't read his inflection.

"How long has the stream's chat been on loop?"

James looked over to his boss, his brows furrowed. "I'm... sorry, sir? I don't know what you mean."

"Aheh... *nice* one, Alton." Slowly looking towards the other man, Daniel's eyes narrowed, ever-so-slowly. "But there's only three direct feeds to the livestream. One's mine, one's on the boat, and the other is *you*. So tell me." Eyes now narrowed to slits, the man leaned close to the camera broadcasting his pilot sphere, mouth curving upwards into a disconcertingly serene smile.

FWOOSH

"Is the stream... *down?*"

James returned the man's gaze. "Sir. With all due respect—I don't think that matters anymore."

"Check it."

"D-Daniel? What's wrong?" Nicki tried to inquire, but Galactic dismissed her with a raised finger as he hissed through his teeth, "James… *check. The. Stream.*"

FWOOSH

Nicki watched James and Daniel stare each other down; over the split screen video, it almost looked as if they were both staring daggers into her very soul. Then at long last, James broke the pseudo-staring contest, and turned to his own secondary monitor.

When Galactic's newest assistant spoke next, his voice was cold, monotonous. "You're right, sir; I'm afraid that the stream does appear to be down. It looks like it's been running through the comments and donations up until the cutoff, and then looping from the beginning."

"Hehehehehehe, yeah…." There was that same raspy laugh again… but Nicki could tell Daniel wasn't crying this time. "You know, I didn't even mention the comments yet… but it is funny in hindsight, right? That the first 'loop' happened *right before* those hands first showed up. I would have thought *someone* would have been more on top of technical difficulties at that point!"

"Sir, I don't know what you're getting at, but I don't appreciate this tone you're taking."

"Really?" Rising out of his chair as much as he could, Daniel's face was practically pressed into the camera lens, to the point where Nicki could visibly watch his skin rapidly turn red as his blood flow increased. "Because *I* think, that you know *exactly* what I'm talking about… you *fucking nigger!*"

"*Daniel!*" Nicki exclaimed, but the irate man cut her off.

"Unless you're going to pull down your *fucking* pants right now and thrust your naked shemale *cock* in the camera for me, I don't want to *fucking hear it!*" Daniel screeched, Nicki clamping a hand over her mouth as James suddenly spiked the camera with a scathing glare.

"*Sir,* do not get a fan involved in this," James commanded, Daniel meeting his gaze with wild eyes.

"Fans?! *Where?* According to the internet, the only fans I know are fucking retarded *children!*" Daniel spat, his expression some horrible in-between of a smile and a scream. "And now, not even those dipshit kids will know where I am, because you and my *fucking two-faced* crew left me off to quietly die at the bottom of the Atlantic *fucking* ocean!"

"Your crew had nothing to do with it. Now *calm yourself.* You're not thinking rationally."

"*Bull-fucking-shit!*" Nicki recoiled as Daniel smashed his fist into the side of the pilot sphere. "I'm thinking more rationally than I ever have in my entire *fucking* career! Because *guess what?!* I've *seen* what happens after this, and it's 'Daniel Kramer' being thrown into some post-mortem video essay *shitheap!* No one worth a single shit will remember what *I* did—it's going to be about fucking *government conspiracies,* or the *one percent,* or my *carpet-munching cunt of a sister!* You've *fucked me,* Alton! You've completely *ass-raped* my entire *fucking* legacy!"

"How could you *say that?!*" Nicki sputtered, feeling as if a gaping hole was being burned into her chest. "I've watched you since the ninth grade! Everyone I *knew* watched you! Any one of us would cite you as a huge inspir—"

"*Boo hoo hoo, you were my chiiiildhood!*" Daniel mock sobbed, rubbing his fists against his eyes. "You're just proving my fucking point! That was *Galactic!* The disposable, flawless fucking paragon that I *had* to play to have any chance of people knowing who I was! I wasn't your fucking babysitter! You didn't know me worth *shit!* And you *couldn't,* because whenever I did what *Daniel* wanted to do, then suddenly I was being labeled 'some degenerate filmschool dropout' or 'a needy, exploitive sexual manipulator,' or a *fucking dyke in drag!*"

Nicki could feel herself trembling as she gripped her remote control, simultaneously barely able to keep watching the video feed, while also terrified of looking anywhere else. "I... I—"

"*Don't you fucking speak!*" Daniel screamed, face completely red with fury. "I became this for *you!* I did *everything* for you! I never asked for *anything,* except to live my fucking life without idiots calling me out for every breath I took! And yet after everything I did, I'm being rewarded by *dying alone* in the name of people who'll forget I exist in a *week,* with my only company being the man who screwed me over and a tranny *whore* who expected *me* to pay *her! I don't pay the sweepstakes winners, you fucking cunt!"*

Almost on instinct, Nicki's finger compressed the red button to brake, her submarine slowing to a stand-still as the thrusters sputtered out. "Wh... why didn't you... then why did you say you would—"

"Because I was hoping to get *laid! Fucking sue me!"* Daniel barked, throwing up his hands. "And there we go, here's my fucking reward *once again!* I change the world on a daily basis, and yet the *one time* I speak out of line, I'm an asshole! Good *fucking* riddance, in what *backwards reality* is *this* the reward I've earned?!"

James had fallen silent as Daniel yelled at Nicki, but with every word, the man's face gradually gave way to open disgust. "This should be the reward for any man like you."

Daniel reacted with an exaggerated gasp, mouth gaping open in a spite-filled half smile. "Oh! *Oooh!* The nigger wants to sass me, does he?! *Sorry* that me being honest hurts your fucking feelings—apparently *you* didn't know me, either!"

"I was told *exactly* who you are, Daniel. This outburst only confirmed the accuracy of my provided information."

"*Really?!* Well did your info-cuck know *this?!"* Daniel hoisted his remote up for the camera and jabbed the tilt button sideways. "Turns out, I'm smart enough not to follow my backhanded assistant into a fucking *death pit* when nobody's watching!" The submarine creaked and groaned as it strained against the water pressure, but Daniel paid it no mind, his eyes locked on James. "Thanks a lot for the damn career eye-opener, Alton! And we'll see 'what I deserve,' when I tell the whole *fucking* internet that you tried conspiring to get the world's *top streamer* killed! Because not to spoil it, but *I* live on, and *you* get forgo—"

Even if Nicki or James had tried, they wouldn't have had time to get out a single word, before Sub 1 ripped itself apart at the seams, instantly compressing The Lord Galactic under fifteen-thousand, seven-hundred fifty pounds of pressure.

"It appears that the colony has begun to settle down."

"...H-huh...?" Nicki finally looked up from her lap, her damp eyes seeming to shimmer in the pilot-sphere's dim lighting. It felt as if she'd been crying for hours, her submarine adrift in the deep sea tunnel the bioluminescent creatures seemed to call home.

James had not slowed. And although his eyes remained fixed on Sub 8's video feed, his voice was genuinely solemn as he addressed the final submarine pilot. "It's not too late to turn back, Nicki. I can tell the extraction team to wait for you."

Nicki's face fell back down into her arms. "I... I can't." She sniffed slightly, her voice muffled against her arms. "This... I-I don't know what this is anymore."

James paused, briefly looking over at the young woman as he considered his words. "This is... a situation that you shouldn't have to concern yourself with."

"Apparently, it really *is!*" Nicki retorted, tears flying

down her face as her head flew up in distress. "I signed up for something I didn't even fully understand, had to watch every other person on the dive *die in front of me,* and it all ended with me learning that my childhood hero was a horrifically racist, homophobic, self-obsessed *maniac!* I should *never* have concerned myself with this—with *him!* I'm just... I'm not... th-there's not even any point...."

James watched Nicki with subdued sympathy, and she stared back at him in turn, her cheeks damp and face a mask of despair. "I apologize if this is personal information, but... do you have family back home, Nicki?"

She shook her head. "My parents disowned me when I first came out," she confessed, pulling her knees close. "I've been living at a friend's house since I turned fifteen."

"I see... and I am sorry in regards to your parents." The older man nodded slowly, setting his jaw. "I can only imagine The Lord Galactic was a source of escape in those days." Nicki didn't comment on this; James exhaled slowly. "It's true we can never really know the creators we follow... but please. Do not use Daniel Kramer as the template for all others in your life."

Nicki laughed hoarsely—it was just as mirthless as the laugh her former idol had let out mere minutes before his death. "James, I... know what you're doing... b-but I don't think you can say that in good faith."

James considered this a moment. "Although I cannot recall them right now, I'm sure there are several sayings about the dangers of blind faith... but. There's also something to be said about distrust, Nicki," he stated plainly; Nicki's eyes drifted back to him, but the man was looking ahead again. "Horrible things have been born when individuals believed others were intrinsically corrupt—often, it's distrust and fear that ultimately *leads* to the blind destruction that so many condemn."

Shifting slightly, Nicki took a long breath... eight seconds in, eight seconds out. "After today... I think trust is going to be easier said than done, knowing there's people like him out there."

"It's better if you remember this day," James interjected, taking Nicki somewhat off-guard. "And you *shouldn't* forget that there are people like him. Because now, you can live your life knowing that, by simply remembering and upholding the morals you watched Daniel discard... you're sincerely becoming the person that he once pretended to be."

The young woman let her head fall back, resting against the back of her chair. She still felt hollow inside. And somehow, she felt that feeling wasn't going to fade for a long while. But hearing James say those words... well, even if she wasn't entirely sure how it made her feel, at least she was feeling something again.

"Do you see yourself as a good person, James?" Nicki questioned, neither of the pilots looking at one another... although, if Nicki had managed to look at the man one last time, she would have seen him shake his head.

"Calling yourself a 'good person' only means that

your views have stagnated," James replied. "That's why I can tell you to go back; because I can admit that what I have to do isn't worth putting an innocent woman through further misery."

"And... what, exactly, do you have to do?"

"I have to put my best foot forward; so that I can keep people like you safe from things that could prove a threat." James smiled coldly to himself, able to tell Nicki was about to say more even without seeing her. "Yes. That is the most you're getting. Any more, and you'll be signing an NDA on the flight back to the states."

"Ha ha...." Nicki laughed quietly—and moments later, to her surprise... she realized her laughter had been genuine. "I... think I understand...."

"I'll allow you forty minutes from now. I can't promise anything beyond that," James informed her, briefly looking over as he tampered with some video settings just out of sight. "God bless you, Nicki. I hope that you can still achieve the life you were seeking today."

"I... I'll try." Nicki nodded slowly, beginning to rotate Sub 12 with her remote. "And... the same goes for you, James." Nicki paused, the submarine suddenly feeling quieter than before. "James?" Her thumb still holding the analog stick, she looked over at the video chat... the feed was now fully dead. "Oh... alright."

Hands shaking, she adjusted her grip on the remote control. Just thirty minutes back—five counting the rotation. She could do this. She... could...

Nicki hadn't noticed it until now, but the sound of the other subs' motors had carried over the video call. Now that she was left to her own devices, it felt as if her ears had just popped after a long flight... and she could hear something that, until now, she hadn't noticed at all.

Breathing.

There it was, finally. It wasn't "traditional" breathing, but the pattern was unmistakable: The slow, rhythmic intake and expulsion of water currents. The absorption of oxygen, and the expulsion of carbon dioxide... it was emanating from all around him. James took a shaky breath, face solemn even as he fought back against his racing heart.

James looked at Sub 9's secondary display, set beside the primary screen utilized for the now-dead video call, and checked on the "stream." Laid over the looping footage of the fabricated Galacti-Chat and accompanying first fifteen minutes of the dive, a tiny icon blinked in and out of view—an icon not visible to any of the other submarine pilots besides James himself. He nodded at the sight—connection to the agency remained secure.

He'd already fulfilled one of the two assignments given to him. And in forty minutes... he would complete his last.

"H-hello? Is someone there?"

Nicki knew she wouldn't get a response—in fact if she *had*, it arguably would have been even worse. But as she laid on her back in that rotated submersible, she was rapidly losing what little power she still held. At that moment, she would have accepted *anything*, instead of the low, rumbling rush of water, rising and falling just beyond where her submarine now idled.

It wasn't the shrimp—her exterior camera picked up no signs of the tiny pinpricks that lined their torsos. As far as present surroundings went, it seemed as if James had been correct in assuming that they had fled the cavern. And it wasn't the unmistakable *"fwoosh"* of a hand coursing through the water. No. *This* was something much, *much* larger. An entity large enough that its breath would shift the water of the cavern back and forth, moving Sub 12 in sync with its oxygen intake.

This realization drained the color from Nicki's face. She *knew* this feeling—the feeling of facing down something beneath the waves, sinking, helpless, into jaws waiting in the darkness far below. Something she couldn't see, but knew all too well was there. She'd lived it time and time again, waking up screaming just before she saw the beast's face. And now, it was here.

Hands quaking, she pressed the analog stick back in the opposite direction. This was her only chance. The creatures could come back any minute. But if she was going to live the life James wanted her to... there was one last thing she needed to face.

Under James Alton's command, Sub 9 drifted further still

from the cavern's entrance. The overwhelming "breath" of the beast remained constant throughout, but after failing to install proper night vision prior to the expedition, James was now counting on that consistency; hearing the reverberations, and the accompanying *squelch* of the creature's flesh, told him of his surroundings.

And what his ears couldn't fill in, the shrimp began to pick up the slack. He could see the unmistakable dots of light again, climbing up and down across the surrounding walls. Even the specimens that seemed to remain stationary still moved, rising and falling in turn with the entity's breathing.

"Additional instances of the unidentified crustaceans have been sighted inside specimen zero." James annunciated every word, concisely and clearly, as his eyes remained on his camera feed. "It is likely that they and the larger specimens—referred to interchangeably as "claws," "arms" or "hands"—have extended their seeming mutualistic relationship towards specimen zero. Benefits of this codependency are unknown, beyond potential shelter."

FWOOSH

"Speak of the devil." James' heart skipped a beat as he heard it—a "claw" flew out of the darkness, floating just over Sub 9. James let it depart, however... his sights were now on the area it had arrived from. His heart heavy in his chest, he accelerated in that direction. "I'm sorry, Cheng... now you see why I didn't want to tie the knot so soon."

Her eyes wide, Nicki stared out at the water. The cavern illuminated by Sub 12's dual spotlights, she slowly panned them up and down the length of the creature before her. Curiosity killed the cat, but in that moment, she was as entranced as she was horrified. She was finally facing the unseen beast that had plagued her mind's eye… the beast that was, at long last, unseen no longer.

Yet, this was no entity meant to be viewed by those beyond the waters it called home. Its slick, reflective body was so large, it pressed against the walls of the cavern. A circular, looming mouth rose before Nicki's eyes, its inner lips adorned with what could only be described as gigantic, rounded teeth. Uncannily *human* teeth, each one at *least* the size of Sub 12, that were sucked in and out as the titanic entity laid in rest, seemingly unaware of Nicki's presence.

Her heart was racing. She couldn't even discern what she was looking at. A massive lamprey? Some disturbingly visceral anemone? Nicki had always been skeptical of alleged beasts that could drive one to madness with just a look. But as she floated barely ten yards from this eyeless monster of the deep, she felt as if her eyes were deceiving her. This couldn't be happening. She was going to wake up any moment now. How could something like *this* have spent centuries undetected by human technology? Did James know about— Nicki's blood went ice cold. *James. He went ahead of me. He's inside of it.*

And in her horror at this realization, Nicki had no time

to react to the creature that then tore from the beast's jaws into the light of the submersible—a creature with a five-pronged head like a horrible claw, each finger covered in clusters of black, rounded eyes over a round, gaping maw, and a tail swaying behind it with countless grasping, prawn-like legs.

She might have screamed when the hellish crustacean punctured the pilot sphere... but in the end, her voice was lost to the ocean's depths.

James grunted as a rush of water pulled the sub forwards. He didn't need to hear nor see the destruction of Sub 12 to realize what was happening—something had alerted specimen zero. It was retracting in as a defense mechanism... and he was now running out of time.

Instinctively James' finger moved to turn the sub, but he caught himself just as quickly. There was no way out now—he knew there likely wouldn't be. And that was *precisely* why they had greenlit this expedition... to access two potential dangers at once.

Water rushing past him, James felt the submarine ricochet off of something beyond his field of view. He could hear the scuttling of unseen shrimp upon impact, the creatures once more rising into a frenzy as the entity they called home went on the alert. Sweat pooling on his face as the steel around him creaked, James took a deep breath. If they wanted clean footage, it was now or never.

James turned on the lights.

And was met with hundreds—perhaps even *thousands* of gruesome shrimp, their sheer numbers almost entirely concealing the innards of the gargantuan anemone they called home. Or rather, as the late pilots had called them, claws, the hulking beasts seemingly being tended to by countless of the smaller, less-developed crustaceans. But James saw now, that they were indeed one and the same, as several of the "hands" recoiled from the wall in a frenzied panic, revealing clusters of large, green eggs clutched to their torsos, their insectoid legs curled inwards like protective cages.

The encroaching threat to the colony announcing its presence with blinding colors, the innumerable males descended upon the steel outsider, their approach compounded as the walls were compressed from every angle. Staring down the multi-eyed crustaceans with nowhere to flee, James spoke one final time, simply and clearly, so as to be absolutely certain his superiors could hear:

"Mission accomplished."

JULY

The Blood Spoon
Michelle Lee

You know when you watch a prank show or video that explicitly exploits your friend's fears? Conversations that follow are usually about what scares you and what doesn't, and sometimes, it leads to questions like, what are you most afraid of out of everything? There's usually a long list of fears and sometimes it's hard to pinpoint only one. My top answers are typically spiders or bugs, snakes, sharks, heights, or earthquakes. That would remain true up until a week ago. My response now would be something that had *never* been on my radar before.

It started with an invitation to a party at a work acquaintance's house. Every job has one of those weird people you tend to shy away from because you get a creepy vibe. Carin was one of those people. I liked to give people the benefit of the doubt, but I couldn't get there with her. I secretly thought she stalked and murdered people with old rusty spoons in her downtime. So when she said she was having a mid-summer school break get-together to celebrate and asked if I wanted to come, my first instinct was to say no adamantly. When I accepted, no one was more surprised than me. I naturally wondered if the event was for her to choose more victims and since I was barely more than civil, I was the perfect choice. I wasn't proud of the thought or how I acted around her.

I didn't go out of my way to treat Carin differently than others. It was more of a gut reaction to keep my distance from her because my danger radar pinged whenever she was around. I couldn't pinpoint why, either. My dislike wasn't that she was weird; everyone is to a certain degree. It wasn't her unattractive hairstyle, dowdy clothing, or funky smell. I couldn't even say the reason was her inconsistent statements, which proved her to be a liar. The only way to sum it up was to call it a bad vibe.

So why did I say I would go? The medical assistants I worked with raised their eyebrows when I agreed to show up, prompting another to agree to attend. I was sure it was nothing more than pure curiosity on their part. Carin disturbed all of us throughout the entire clinic, with no exceptions. Maybe we all wanted to see where she lived and what the décor of a sociopath was. That was another of those thoughts that made me question my niceness as a person.

"Did I have a stroke, or did you agree to go to Carin's party?" Shannon, one of the medical assistants, asked me after Carin walked away. "And why did I say I'd go?"

"Momentary lapse in judgment?" I shrugged. "I'm

glad you are going, so there will be a witness if she tries to murder me. We should bring people we know we can outrun," I added wryly as an afterthought.

"Carin only has an adult-aged kid, so why is she having mid-summer school break party?" Shannon wondered, crossing her arms and tapping her finger on her chin.

"That's your only question?" I asked sarcastically. "You should be questioning why we are attending."

We returned to work and maintained a distance from Carin as much as possible in the small clinic. We saw her entering the exam rooms more than once, which was odd since she worked at the reception desk and had no reason to be there. She'd slink around the corner as if we couldn't see a person enter the room, and come out a few minutes later with an expression that gave me chills. I put it out of my mind because I had more things to worry about than Carin.

The approaching party loomed over my head like the Gods of the old worlds issued an ominous warning that I had made a terrible mistake. I couldn't, in all fairness, say that the warning was wrong since Shannon said something similar to me in passing on a busy day in the clinic.

"Backing out now gives Carin all the power," I whispered to Shannon in the hallway by the breakroom. "We'll look like chicken shits."

"Hmm," Shannon hummed with a sarcastic tone. "Bravery, or being murdered by the clinic psycho serial killer?

Did the mole on her face get bigger?"

I laughed quietly. "Why are you looking that closely? And do you feel like a mean girl right now? I do."

"I mean, kinda." Shannon shrugged. "Carin asked me how my weekend was earlier today and I said it was busy. She told me she saw that and hoped I got some sleep. What was that supposed to mean? I swear I shivered when she said that."

I shuddered at the implication. "Are you bringing your husband with you? Mine refuses."

"So did mine! He told me there was no way in hell he would step foot voluntarily in her house. I even tried to bribe him with special favors." Shannon shook her head. "I even played the what if I die card. He told me to make sure my life insurance was current so he could get a nanny to watch the kids."

I laughed again. "I played the die card too. He told me that this wasn't a Romeo and Juliet thing and I shouldn't expect him to die with me when it was my own stupidity that put me in the situation to begin with."

"Ugh. This is what happens when I eavesdrop on a conversation without proper caffeination in the morning," Shannon sighed. "We need another person to go with us. Jessica likes horror stories, think she'd come?"

The problem was no one liked Carin. No one wished her harm either, but getting someone to join us at a party at her house stretched the limits of friendships. Something was so off with this woman that you didn't even want to be in the same room as her at work, where you got a paycheck for being there.

"Get Jessica to do what?" Jessica asked as she snuck up behind us. "Watch out, the creepy stalker is watching you from around the corner."

"Yeah," Shannon drawled with an evil smile. "You should come with us to a party on Saturday. We can have a girl's day."

"As fun as that sounds, the look on your face and hers," Jessica nodded at me, "tells me that there is something else going on here. Why is Carin so creepy?" she whispered the question. "She's totally peeking around the corner like her pale, day glow skin doesn't stand out."

Shannon snickered. I kept my back facing the direction where Carin hid. "Remember a couple of weeks ago when Carin cornered me? She asked me to go to her party and my dumb ass agreed to go. Then Shannon, in her brilliance, agreed to go as well. We need more backup."

"Are you fu..." Jessica's voice trailed off before she finished the curse because a patient walked out of a room. "Are you serious?"

"Yeah," I admitted sheepishly. "I don't know what possessed me because I intended to say no."

"She's not lying," Shannon backed me up. "I was watching her face and it showed disdain. I swore I had a stroke when I heard her voice say sure. Then it was like whatever possessed her got me because I agreed. I think she hexed us."

"And now you want me to join your insanity?" Jessica hissed. "Eh, what the hell, I'll go. If nothing else, it'll get my heart rate up and my watch will think I'm working out. What are you going to wear?"

"Sparkly bulletproof body armor," Shannon muttered. "With running shoes."

"For sure, running shoes," Jessica agreed. "What kind of party is this anyway?"

"Mid-summer school break party," I quoted Carin. Before I could say anything else, Jessica shushed me.

"She's coming this way," Jessica warned. "Did you order more urine cups?" Jessica asked Shannon. Jessica kept her body language and tone the same as before the warning.

"I did; they'll be here before the end of the week," Shannon confirmed. "We should have enough to get by. I stashed a few in the extra room if we run out."

"Thanks," Jessica straightened and walked away. "Back at it."

Shannon nodded and we all separated before Carin got close. I beelined for the bathroom to avoid conversation and locked the door, leaning against it in relief. There was something very wrong about Carin and it made my skin crawl.

Shannon and Jessica sat next to me at work for lunch on Friday. "Where do you want to meet?" Jessica asked. "I'm just assuming that we all want to head into the devil's den together at the same time and as a unified front."

I couldn't help it; I laughed heartily at the description. It was funny because it was true. I'd also had the same thought and had been trying to figure out a good meeting place for all of us. We all lived south, but Jessica was the closest to me.

"We can meet here," I suggested. "Or Jessica can come to my house and park, and I can drop down the hill to get you, Shannon."

"I might have to meet you," Shannon mused. "I think I have something going on earlier in the day with my daughter. I can't remember. I've been too tired and now worried to think about it."

"Are we supposed to bring anything?" I asked softly. I didn't want anyone else to overhear our conversation. Not that anyone would rat us out to Carln.

"I don't know," Shannon whispered back. "I'm afraid to eat anything she makes. She'd probably poison us with something that will slowly eat away at our insides so we die a painful death."

"For sure," Jessica agreed readily. "We'd bleed from our eyes, too."

"So macabre," I giggled. "I don't disagree, though."

"I'll pick you up," Jessica told me, getting back on topic. "We can meet Shannon here and she can drive us. Her vehicle is bigger and she can ram it through the house if she needs to when things go sideways. I'm fully expecting that's the direction we will go after we arrive."

"That's the way to think positive!" Shannon

exclaimed. "You aren't wrong though."

"Definitely bring your own drink that's sealed," I said as an afterthought.

The temperature in the breakroom dropped a couple of degrees, enough for all three of us to notice the difference. As we finished eating, we rubbed the pebbled skin on our arms, and then Carin walked in. A calculating gaze swept over us, and a different chill went down my spine this time.

"Ladies," Carin greeted us. "It's been quite a day today."

"Busy as usual," Shannon said, kicking me under the table. "I hate you," she mumbled under her breath to me.

No one said anything else until Carin walked out the back door and we were positive there was no chance she could hear anything we said. We watched as she got in her vehicle and stared at us from behind the steering wheel of her car.

"Okay. I'm uncomfortable," I muttered. "And it's not my fault you said you'd go. You jumped in with that on your own."

"I know, but it's more fun to blame you," Shannon replied with a frown.

The day of the party arrived and I stood in my closet looking at my clothes. "What do I want to die in?" I asked myself. My husband wasn't home, so I didn't get to ask his opinion. His parting remark before leaving for my uncle's house was to leave a description of the clothes I was wearing on the counter so he knew what to tell the police I had on when I went missing. He was a funny man.

I finally picked out a pair of comfortable jeans and a sarcastic t-shirt that declared I lost interest. Was it mean? Probably. Did I feel bad? Not in the least. I wasn't interested in Carin's life or want her as a friend. The frightening vibe she put off was noticed by more than me, and I felt it was in my best interest and safety to keep her at a distance. I didn't set out to make her feel bad, but I wasn't open with her either.

I went downstairs to wait for Jessica and smiled at the squirrel in my backyard begging for food. The day was bright, beautiful, and a perfect summer day. The temperature wasn't too hot yet, though it would head that way later in the afternoon. With that in mind, I put on a pair of sandals that had buckles so if I had to run, I could, without tripping over my shoes.

I heard Jessica honk from the front and grabbed my purse and keys. I waved to her as I locked the front door, swallowed my fear, and went to get in. I saw she was dressed similarly to me and felt a smidgen better about my choices.

"Are you scared?" Jessica asked as we turned around and headed to work to meet Shannon. "I can't shake this weird feeling."

"Yeah," I confirmed. "I've got it too. It's almost like going to a haunted house at Halloween, but not fun."

"Yes!" Jessica thumped her steering wheel.

"Exactly."

"We'll be fine. All three of us are badass in our different ways," I told Jessica, trying to convince both of us.

"Oh, we'll be fine," Jessica assured me strongly and defiantly. "That scrawny sociopath won't take us easily. I'm sure that something will happen, though. It's that not knowing that has me on edge. I don't have any clue what we are walking into."

"I left the address where we are supposed to be on the counter," I confided.

"I did, too," Jessica said with a laugh. "I told my son to text me every hour and if I don't reply, to send the police to that address."

We fell silent as Jessica drove, and it felt like no time had passed before we pulled in next to Shannon. She had on a glittery tank top, which made me laugh. I hopped out of Jessica's vehicle and waved. Shannon looked as nervous as we did.

"Where's the body armor?" I asked with a smile.

"Trust me, I considered it," Shannon replied. "This feels like a mistake."

"I agree." I shook my head as Jessica locked her vehicle. "Jessica and I were talking about how this feels like we are going to a not-fun haunted house."

"No." Shannon shook her head. "Even the bad haunted houses, or real ones, are more fun than this. I don't have words for the feelings inside me."

"Why are we doing this then?" Jessica asked. "Who's

idea was it?"

"I agreed to go, which wasn't my intention," I reminded her. "Then, out of nowhere, Shannon said she'd go."

"You two are insane," Jessica muttered. "Let's get this over with. Shotgun."

I chuckled and got in the back of the big SUV. I had to admit the size did give me some comfort about fleeing if we had to. I handed Shannon the paper with the address and watched as she punched it into the GPS on her dash. It was anticlimactic when no doom music played.

I noted that each of us had an unopened water bottle and grinned despite the butterflies in my stomach. We didn't bring food, which might have been a mistake, but I didn't think I'd be able to eat anyway. My stomach was a mess.

"Do you think anyone other than us will be there?" Shannon wondered.

"I have no idea," I mumbled. "I can't imagine who. We'll find out."

"What if it's a trap because we are bitchy to her?" Jessica tossed out. "We could be her prey."

"Like I hadn't thought about that already." Shannon smirked. "I want to think that she isn't as bad as we think she is, but some of the doctors we work with shudder when she's around and they are the nicest people ever."

I felt the same way. Not that I wanted to be a bitch or think of myself that way, but I tended to see people in a pleasant light first. That hadn't happened with Carin. The moment I met her, I wanted to be as far away from her as possible.

"Well, damn," Jessica retorted. "We're only a minute away."

The tension in the vehicle rose as we approached an older-style home with Carin's car parked in the driveway. The house was light brown with dying grass in the front yard. The shrubs and plants looked like torture was their care routine before they gave up and withered. The driveway was mossy and had several large cracks that buckled parts of it. To be fair, most houses on the street looked the same, only with better landscaping. However, the street was unnaturally still and quiet. Not even crows were hanging around.

"I can't comment on the yard work since mine would look that way if I had a yard," I said, trying to put a positive spin on it. "I don't understand the windows, though."

"I think they have a reflective tint to them," Shannon said. She parked on the street with her vehicle facing the way we would have to leave. I knew it was intentional and was happy she did it.

"Okay, y'all." Jessica looked at each of us before we opened the doors. "I'm a bitch. If she's going after someone, it will be me first." She said it with a matter-of-fact tone that left no room for argument. "I correct her all the time and point out her mistakes."

"You aren't a bitch," I told her. "Knock it off. I don't think Carin has the balls to outright go after anyone." That was my sincerest hope of the day.

"No," Shannon agreed. "She'd be sneaky about it, which is why I said she'd poison us. Do you know how many murder podcasts I listen to? I totally have her pegged."

"Come on, then," Jessica said bravely. She opened the door and slid out of her seat like reluctant molasses on a frozen winter morning.

Shannon and I followed, and as a trio, we slowly walked toward the front door. The temperature outside was about ninety degrees by then, but as we neared the house, it felt like the air was chilled, as if we were standing under an air conditioning vent. There were no trees overhead and the house was in direct sunlight. It didn't make sense.

"Hello, ladies." Carin opened the door before we arrived on the porch. "Oh, Jessica, hello. I wasn't expecting you. Nice to see you. The more the merrier." Her smile made my stomach roll like turbulent thunder. I also noted she dressed the same way she did for work.

Four million invisible spiders crawled over my body at her tone. I repressed a shudder and forced a smile on my face. Even a blind person could see it wasn't real. "Hi, Carin," I greeted her. My tone was off and it showed my nervousness. I didn't even sound like me.

"Come in." Carin held the door open for us. Behind her was nothing but darkness. It was another anomaly that didn't make sense since it was early afternoon and the sun was blinding.

I glanced at the windows again, unsettled because I couldn't see inside through them or the open door. I supposed it was just as well. When we stepped in, it felt like we were back in the seventies. Super long shag carpet in that orange-brown color covered the floor, and on it sat corduroy furniture covered in clear plastic, with floral and paisley throw pillows. Doilies peppered the tables, and the walls had an odd yellow tinge that spoke of age like nicotine coated the surface.

I looked back at the windows and let out a little sigh of relief that I could see outside at least. Then I noticed the golden floral-print black-out curtains hanging on either side of the window. Carin was watching me take in everything.

"The furniture is my ex's. Since it was free, I haven't bothered to change anything," Carin explained in a monotone voice. "The house doesn't have any shade, so I had the tint put on the windows to help with the summer heat. Oddly, it helps keep the heat in during the winter. Those hundred-degree days we had were terrible, so I was thankful for the black-out curtains. It kept it to eighty degrees inside."

Shannon moved a step closer to me. "I can see how those would help. Good idea."

"Uh, yeah," Jessica agreed and moved closer to Shannon. "My house is older, too. I'll have to look into those curtains. It feels cool in here now." Jessica gave a surreptitious look around while maintaining a blank expression on her typically expressive face. If I hadn't felt so creeped out I would have laughed.

Likewise, Carin showed no facial tells of what she was

thinking. "Yeah. They're great."

The disassociated stare had me on edge, and if Shannon had not linked her arm through mine, I would have bolted. "Are we going to sit outside and enjoy the weather?" I asked, my voice squeaking.

"Oh, no." Carin shook her head. "I'm too fair for that. I'd burn. I thought we could use the add-on room I paid to build earlier this year. You'll be the first company to see it."

I heard Shannon gulp. I figured she would bring us to that room, but instead, Carin stood there and stared at us some more. I don't remember a time when I felt more uncomfortable than I did at that moment.

"Okay," Jessica drawled, breaking the silence. "Lead the way. We'll follow you."

"Oh. Right." Carin turned and slowly walked toward the back of the house.

Not one of us moved to follow. We all looked back at the front door with longing. "How is this my life?" Shannon hissed in my ear.

"You volunteered!" I reminded her with a frantic whisper.

"This way, ladies," Carin called out to us. "I think you'll like it. The others are already in there waiting."

"Others?" Jessica elbowed me. "What others? There are no cars outside."

She had a point. The street had been empty when we pulled up. There weren't even cars in the driveways of the neighboring houses. That meant there was no one around to hear us scream. *Why was my brain so set on us dying here?*

"Come on!" Shannon pulled us. "We have to follow her."

"Do we?" Jessica questioned caustically.

"Yes!" Shannon's emphatic answer was puzzling. "I need to see these other friends."

I swallowed a laugh and forced my feet to move. We followed Carin through a stark white kitchen that looked straight out of time but unused. Everything was white—the cupboards, appliances, countertops, floor, furniture, and blinds. Come to think of it, I didn't even smell the scent of food prepared for a party. I only smelled the scent of old, like when you walked into a second-hand store.

We went through a dark and windowless narrow hallway and came to a heavy closed door. How did I know it was heavy? It took Carin some effort to open it. An odd thought occurred to me after she stepped into the room. She only opened the door enough for her to slip through as if she were trying to keep something inside.

"Hey guys, the rest of the group is here," Carin said.

Shannon pulled me along with her as she stepped through the door. I heard her frightened gasp and followed her in with Jessica behind me. I didn't process the scene in front of me right away. Instead, my hand snatched the keys sitting on the top of Shannon's open purse and stuffed them in my pocket. There was no way I wanted them to drop or get taken and not have a way out of there.

"What the actual fuck?" Jessica retorted in

astonished horror. She didn't bother to quiet her tone. It was a sentiment I agreed with.

Before us was a folding table covered with a red and white checked vinyl tablecloth; around the table were six folding chairs, and in four of the chairs sat a mannequin—rather, what used to be a dummy. These figures had strands of hair in random places on their bald heads as if they had been glued or threaded into the material, which made them look like they had undergone several rounds of chemotherapy.

Odd patches of what looked like eyelashes, or perhaps pubic hair, were clumped over some of the eyes and makeup had been haphazardly applied to faces. I would rather sit at a table with a killer clown holding red balloons. That was when I noticed that the positioned hands on the table had pieces of fingernails glued to the fingertips.

"Oh, dear," Carin groaned. "I'm missing a chair. I wasn't expecting Jessica, but that's okay. I can run and get another chair. Feel free to take a seat and get to know the others."

With a sidelong look at Shannon and Jessica, I saw their faces reflecting the fear I felt building inside my body at an increasing pace. Our feet froze to the floor; I shifted my gaze around the room, looking for escape routes or possible weapons to defend against an attack. *But from what? A mannequin?*

"Is that real hair?" Shannon whispered in horror.

"Does that mean you haven't noticed the fingernails

or eyelashes yet?" Jessica hissed back.

"Oh, my God," I said. "That's what she's been doing in the exam rooms!" The pieces quickly fell into place in my mind and I hoped against all sanity that I wasn't right. "She's collecting them."

"Grody!" Shannon exclaimed. "Why? That makes me feel violated!"

"Why, what?" Carin asked as she heaved a wooden chair into the room. The heavy door closing behind her with the sound of finality jolted each of us. "I'm so angry." Carin's monotone voice sent a spike of adrenaline rushing through my veins. "I told him to stay away today. It was supposed to be a girl's day. But no, he has to come back. He's always spying on me. It was his idea for me to have a get-together. Well, too bad for him, he's not getting in here."

Carin bolted the door closed with a key she produced from her pocket. When she slid it back into the pocket, it felt like all hope had disappeared from the room. A chill descended from the ceiling and soaked into my bones. I felt Shannon and Jessica shivering next to me, so it wasn't a figment of my overactive imagination.

"Did you introduce yourselves?" Carin asked as she dragged the chair to the table, making room for one more. "This lovely lady is Susan. Next to her, we have Amanda, then Julie, and finally Alyssa. Ladies, these are the gals from work I've been telling you about."

She didn't introduce us. We remained rooted in place while Carin had an entire, one-sided conversation with the mannequins. She talked about the plastic toy food on the plates before them and acted like a wonderful hostess.

"There are teeth in the corner," Jessica whispered. "What is happening?"

"Voodoo," Shannon answered. "She's trying to make voodoo dolls. Look closer. Each mannequin has holes where she has stuck them with something." The fact that pointed chopstick-looking things lie on the table supported her theory.

"What if we are imagining this?" I asked quietly. "It's not real."

"Keep saying that." Jessica frowned at me. "Maybe you'll eventually believe it. We are in a circle of hell right now. Trapped."

"Look." Shannon nodded to a couple of tables with candles, dark bowls, skulls, and other things I couldn't identify.

"But that is just stuff that people think is associated with voodoo or witchcraft. It doesn't mean it's real," I argued. I didn't know how to explain the metallic blood smell that rose in the air.

"Whether it's real or not, Carin believes it is, and we walked right into it. We need not to touch anything," Shannon warned.

"Sit," Carin commanded us, the jovial tone she'd used with the dummies gone. An acrid smell reached my nostrils and burned through my lungs.

It was as if my feet had a mind of their own and

began to move toward one of the folding chairs. Carin had placed a mannequin on each side of an empty chair, forcing us apart and placing the creepy figures between us. I'd hoped my instincts about Carin were wrong, but I was foolish and naive.

I heard Jessica's phone vibrate and sent up a desperate prayer that her son would call for help when she didn't respond. My heart thudded in my chest, and my head was feeling foggy. I smelled the candles burning and wondered when she lit them and if that was what made me feel dizzy. I didn't want to entertain the idea of a gas filling the room.

As Shannon warned, I kept my hands on my lap and touched nothing. My gaze flickered between my two friends and Jessica looked angry but her eyes were wild and caged. Shannon's eyes reflected the dancing flame of a candle and seemed empty. That worried me and I tried to kick her but couldn't feel my legs.

I heard a disembodied voice about that time, though I couldn't tell you where it came from or if I hallucinated it. I couldn't tell you anything at all about what was happening. I didn't know. I couldn't speak and I refused to move. It felt like my will was getting suppressed, as if something were taking me over.

Somewhere behind me, Carin happily hummed as she moved about, breaking up the annoying sound with random chatter aimed at the dummy friends. My eyes were getting heavier and I watched in horror as Carin clipped off a piece of hair from Shannon and Jessica both. Seconds later, my eyes closed no matter how hard I tried to keep them open.

I came to consciousness with a flare of pain like lightning in my skull. My head snapped forward and thumped into the seat before me. I grunted and rubbed my head, my hand feeling sticky and wet. I blinked a few times to get my eyes in focus and saw I was back in Shannon's SUV. My vision wasn't clear but I could see enough of the shapes to tell where I was. Shannon and Jessica were in the front seats. The vehicle remained parked outside Carin's house.

"What the hell?" I mumbled. My tongue felt swollen and thick, my throat was dry, and my lungs ached. In fact, my entire body hurt. *Where was my bottle of water?* I fumbled my hand around blindly on the floor, feeling for the plastic container, but my eyes still weren't seeing clearly.

"Wha—?" Jessica tried to speak.

"Thirsty," Shannon muttered a few seconds later.

Did we have heat stroke? How long were we out here? I had brief flashes of memories that didn't make sense and my head was pounding relentlessly. My flailing hand finally bumped into the water bottle and I grasped it firmly as if I were afraid it would disappear. I'm not sure how I managed to get the cap off, but I did and took a giant swallow before handing the bottle up between Shannon and Jessica.

"Drink," I told them, my voice faint.

My limbs were weak, and I felt relieved when Jessica took the bottle from me. If she could do that, she would be okay. I blinked a few more times to try and get my eyes clear enough to see in focus. When my vision returned, I stared in shock as Jessica ran her hands over her face and saw the blood.

I fumbled in my purse for my phone and got the screen on. I pulled up my camera app and looked at my face. It, too, was red with smeared blood. That was all it took to get my senses back into focus and in the present. Shock value at its best.

"Shannon. Drink some water and get with it. We need to leave now!" I demanded frantically. I didn't know if we had open wounds anywhere that needed attention. If we did, this wasn't the location to address it.

My tone got through to her and I watched her jerky movements as she guzzled the rest of the water down. My veins felt like they were vibrating and my head thumped in time with my racing heartbeat. Adrenaline raced through me like wildfire.

"Did we go in?" Jessica asked dazedly. The usual spark in her tone was non-existent.

"I think so and that's why we need to leave now," I repeated. "We are covered in blood. Start the car and get off this street."

Shannon yanked the rearview mirror down to look at herself and shrieked. That was all it took. The vehicle roared to life and we peeled off down the road and around the corner with the squeal of rubber on the pavement. I thought she would stop but she didn't until we pulled back into the parking lot at work.

We stared at each other in silence. I was desperately trying to remember what happened and each time I thought I had a hold on a memory, blinding pain hit right behind my eyes and I lost it. We had a chunk of hair missing from all our heads and someone, Carin presumably, clipped our nails. I couldn't remember why that was significant.

"We aren't going to speak of this," Shannon ordered. "Go home. Shower as often as we need to, and we move on." Fear laced every word she said. I wondered if she remembered anything.

Neither Jessica nor I argued. We got out of the vehicle and into hers. The drive back was silent except for one question. "Do you remember anything?" Jessica asked. All I could do was shake my head no. Her lips pursed and she shook her head at my questioning gaze.

After she dropped me off, I went into the house, straight upstairs, removed all my clothes, threw them in the garbage can, and showered. I scrubbed my skin until it was pink and raw. I found a cut on my hand, but that didn't account for the amount of blood covering my face, neck, hands, and wrists. Several spots on my body had the appearance of a beginning bruise. I gathered my favorite lotion, covered myself with the soothing scent, crawled into bed, and hid.

Parts of memories returned to me in my sleep, though they were jumbled and didn't make sense. My husband couldn't rouse me and he left me alone after assuring himself I was physically intact. He assumed I didn't feel well, which was true. I slept almost the entire next day as well. I did manage to send texts checking on Shannon and Jessica. The answers were short and succinct, letting me know they were alive.

Monday, I got up for work. My movements were disjointed and I wondered if I were getting a summer flu. I didn't have a fever, so I went anyway. Shannon and Jessica were there already, and we stared at each other with a thousand questions on our faces that we had never given a voice to.

Jessica walked into the building, gathered up all her things, hugged me, hugged Shannon, and left without a backward look. Shannon shook her head at me and showed me a letter she'd drafted requesting immediate transfer to another location and that she wouldn't be in the clinic until it happened.

Following their actions, I sat down and wrote out my notice. I left it on my supervisor's desk and cited mental health reasons as to why I would no longer be working there. Shannon and I left at the same time that Carin pulled into the parking lot.

"I can't," Shannon whispered, her eyes wide with fear. "Things are coming back. I need to go."

"Same," I replied. I hugged Shannon and we got in our respective vehicles and left. We never saw Carin again. I believed she could find us because something had happened to all three of us, and none of us knew what that was. We all found spoons in our purses with the handle end filed into a knife point, with the tip covered in blood.

So, what am I afraid of, you might wonder? Spoons and mannequins.

august

Paradise

Joe Nasta

avid didn't want to wake up again.

Welcome to Paradise! The pamphlet made it seem like every participant would be satisfied forever inside the simulation—it would be tailored to match his personal taste. Before uploading his consciousness to the server, he had taken a standardized test in a large lecture hall filled with desks. He was the only person in the room aside from a proctor in a white lab coat stationed at the front.

There were one hundred and seventy five questions.

What's your favorite city?

    a.   Palm Springs

    b.   Pheonix

    c.   Portland

    d.   Pittsburgh

Which color?

    a.   Periwinkle

    b.   Puce

    c.   Peach

    d.   Purple

What are you searching for?

a.   Passion

b.   Purpose

c.   Pleasure

d.   Peace

It all seemed very scientific to David.

He sat in the middle of the front row and bubbled his answers in with a pencil. When he was done, the proctor took his answer sheet and instructed him to remain seated. They told him that once his data had been processed in the system, the program would have enough information to personalize the simulation. The entire process would only take fifty-five seconds, but the machine was kept in a secure offsite-location. It would take a few minutes to drive over there. Luckily, David was a very patient man and wasn't in a rush.

He settled into the hard chair and savored the last moments of corporeal discomfort he would ever feel again. The Paradise Program Coordinators had told him to fast for two full days before onboarding, so he was hungry and dehydrated. A sharp pinpoint headache persisted in each temple and a knot churned in his small intestine.

About an hour later, one short man with a mustache and one tall man wearing square glasses, both in white coats, escorted him down the hall, into an elevator, and down into the basement. The space stretched into the distance. The dim blue lighting was insufficient to see how far. The aisles were lined with translucent capsules sharped like sarcophaguses, all empty. This is where his body would be kept.

David had heard about the giveaway on Instagram. One of his high school acquaintances that he didn't speak to any more had tagged him and three other of their classmates. Since he hadn't heard from any of these people in years, it felt something like fate. The post was AI generated with that unreal shimmer that lifted off the phone screen, making the pomegranate-colored tagline even more appealing: Pioneer Paradise.

Everything in his life had gone wrong and he was ready for something new. More than change he wanted to leave everything else behind: His ex and her new husband, the job he was laid off from, the friends he'd burned bridges with, the new crowd he'd begun hanging out with but was afraid to commit to. He daydreamed about his own little world without stress or messy feelings. He filled out the entry form on Paradise's website, hit submit, and went back to watching Netflix.

Now he was here. It happened quickly, only a week between entering and signing the papers. He was going to be the first person to leave his body behind.

The short mustached man pressed some buttons on the panel and the pod opened.

"Get in," the tall man with glasses said. David did as he was told.

More buttons. Four metal prongs slid into his skull from different angles, then shifted so his neck was slightly bent forward. Without warning, a fifth prong ejected from the back of the pod and into his brainstem: the upload would begin shortly.

A puff of sedative gas rushed in from the air filtration unit and a gooey fluid rushed in from the pipes installed at the bottom of the pod. It made him shiver as the level rose over his feet, up his calves, around his waist. His lower extremities began to numb. The men watched silently as the flesh that used to be David began to go limp. Finally, submerged all the way to his neck in the clear paste and falling into a coma, the body was ready for the parting.

The process was irreversible. It had only ever been conducted on lab rats, but he'd signed the waiver. When his consciousness began to tear away from his bones, it clung to the sinew. A gentle sucking from the cord in the back of his neck grew and the connection between his essence and his physical form peeled away until only a thread ran from who David was to what he had been before. Right in the center of his chest, the last bit of rubber keeping him tied to reality stretched, thinned, snapped.

David didn't want to wake up again.

Every day was the same. It was always that specific part of late August when the dog days broke but it wasn't yet fall. He had explored every part of Paradise and wanted a way out. Time had no meaning. Maybe it had been a few days, or maybe it had been a few years, he had so quickly lost track. David was the only person in his simulation as his test results had indicated he would be most happy by himself. Now he didn't want to be alone but it was too late.

The alarm went off at exactly 7:30 am. The kitchen table was set with all of his favorite breakfast foods. The sky outside the skylight was partially cloudy and on the verge of drizzle, which was his ideal weather. The live in Central Park recording of "A Heart in New York" by Art Garfunkel came on the speaker as he munched on bacon and hard boiled eggs, which he did every so-called morning.

He went for a walk. The main street was populated with a coffee shop, an Ace Hardware store, a Whole Foods, a pizza restaurant, a Buffalo Exchange thrift store, and a dive bar because these were the ideal establishments that would fulfill his every need. When he walked in, everything he could possibly desire was already set up for him—the artisanal cheese, farfalle pasta, and Alfredo sauce he had a hankering for already in the shopping basket next to the conveyor belt, a breve latte steaming on the counter with just the right amount of foam, three slices of pepperoni hot out of the oven on a paper plate, or a Manny's Pale Ale in a frozen glass—without so much as him saying a word.

David didn't remember the last time he had spoken aloud. Sometimes the rats would peek their heads out of sewers and he would try to talk to them, but they scurried away before he could work up the courage.

At the time the simulation pretended was afternoon, there was a thunderstorm. He had always loved when they arrived, the release in barometric pressure and anticipation they brought with them. When he was young, he would count the seconds between the lightning strike and the booming sound that followed, divide by seven to calculate how many miles away he was from the eye of the storm.

Each day he waited in the park for the rain to come. The clouds moved in their predictable formations and the darkness creeped in. The drops broke out of them and smacked his skin, picked up speed and frequency. Then the spectacular spark and a crack! He almost felt alive.

But here the storm was unnatural. The rain, the light, the thunder all started at precisely 4:45 pm. There was no delay, no distance. Paradise was always at the center. Everything revolved around David and he couldn't stand it. He missed everyone.

Then something changed; at the center of town a large brick building with a grand staircase leading up to an intricate oak wood door had appeared. The features of the building were intricately detailed with granite and marble. At the apex of the pointed roof a gargoyle perched to watch over Paradise.

He was shocked. He had never seen anything change here. The clouds had disappeared and it remained sunny well into the late afternoon. His rain, lighting, thunder did not come. The temperature reached 85 degrees—much too warm. Was someone else finally coming? Had someone realized he was gone and investigated his disappearance, following the tracks of legal paperwork and coded social media posts to the basement where his body sat immersed in goo? Did someone love him enough to upload themselves to the Paradise they would share together for eternity?

Excited, he went to the thrift store and found a new T-shirt that not only fit exactly right but had his favorite Looney Tunes character emblazoned on the back! How lucky. He wanted to get a good night's rest so he went to bed early wearing his new favorite shirt.

David was thrilled to wake up again. Today vines began to grow in front of the brick building, stretching the length of the staircase and rooting between the bricks as it scaled the front facade. He carefully approached, testing each step as he fingered the leaves. Red grapes were beginning to form, so he pulled one off and popped into his mouth: too sour, not yet ripe. What a thrill that something was growing in Paradise.

The gargoyle peered down at him as he knocked on the door. No answer. He tried the knob—locked. This was the only locked door he'd come across in the simulation. David began to wonder who he was waiting for, who was going to join him. He imagined his ex-wife, his estranged brother, a man he met at the corn hole league the month before he crossed over, the barista he used to see every Wednesday morning, the clerk who supervised the self-checkout lanes at the grocery store, a family having a picnic in the grass and playing on the swings in the park, a stranger sitting down the bar from him once and never again, that pretty girl he swiped right on but didn't match with, a bus driver who nodded as he paid the fare. He remembered everyone and he missed them all too damn much.

Time passed again. The sun stayed out. Nobody new came. The grapes spoiled, then fell off the vine. The lab rats scurried around the base of the grand staircase. The park was becoming overgrown with weeds and not even a vintage tour shirt for an indie band he liked could cheer him up.

David didn't want to wake up again.

But he had a plan. He was going to find out what was in the brick building, what the gargoyle was hiding from him. Those watchful eyes that at first seemed caring, hopeful, and all-knowing now filled him with rage.

He went to the hardware store. As always what he needed was already there. Today it was an ax and a utility belt. He grabbed them and hurried to the brick building, climbing the stairs two at a time. He strapped the ax to his waist and began to climb up the vines.

The coarse stems and hardened blooms hurt his hands. He couldn't remember the last time he had felt so physical. About halfway up the building his palm tore and began to bleed. At the top David mantled up onto the roof and stood up next to his enemy.

He shouted, the rasp of his voice emerging after so long as his mouth struggled to shape the sound into discernible words, "Help! Help! Let me out!"

The gargoyle didn't move or answer. The sun beat down and David's sweat bled into his simulated eyes. He raised the ax and swung, beating the statue until it cracked open and pieces fell towards the ground below. In his fury, his feet lost grip on the roof and then he was falling with them. The grey stone and gargoyle wings and his eyes were all hurled downward. As he twisted midair and waited for the inevitable crash, he realized being alive hadn't been so bad after all.

It was 7:30 again in Paradise. The alarm went off. David woke up.

September

Light

Marie Locker

My eyes are wide. I did not know my eyes could go this wide. I cannot look away. What am I even looking at? I try to calm my breathing, but the only thing making that semi possible is this heavy feeling I have, like I am underneath a weighted blanket. *What is this thing?* I cannot scream. There is this thick, nothing in my throat that prevents me from uttering anything above a whimper. This thing is just there. A black mass of a person in my bed. Are they staring at me?

I feel like hours go by staring at this thing, and the whole time I am trying to scream, move, make any kind of noise. I am terrified. I can see the black, rounded shoulders moving like it is breathing. I try to let myself think and move one body part at a time. *Try your fingers!* My panicked mined races. I put all my concentration into moving my fingers, something, anything to gain control of the situation. Nothing. I can't move! How is this possible? I must have been drugged. *You live alone!* I think to myself. I feel the tears start welling up and running down the side of my face. I can feel the pillow beneath me start to get saturated and warm. How could I feel all of this, but I can't move or make any noise? It does not make sense to me. I shut my eyes tight, hoping this would help either make this thing do whatever it came here to do, and get it over with, or it would disappear. I open my eyes. It's still there.

I think I surrendered—something inside surrendered. At least, that's the last thing I remember before coming to. I closed my eyes gently, and then slowly came back into the conscious realm. I woke up. The feeling of feeling coming back one limb at a time. Sweat beads on my forehead mimic the dew beads I see on the plants outside my window, the perfect September morning. I sit up, look back in my bed, and see my body outlined in my own sweat. "This was too close this time" I mutter to myself, gathering my sheets so I can wash them.

Still worried but trying to calm myself down from the nightmare I had, I try to make sense of what these dreams are doing to me. I am terrified of going to sleep—or as my therapist is naming it, I have Somniphobia—because of these nightmares. "Shit!" I say, startling myself, the soap overflowing the dispenser for the laundry. "Get yourself together, Michelle," I mutter.

My therapist is going to love this. She doesn't believe me about these nightmares. No, she is more concerned she can cure me from my "fear of the dark", and again she has properly diagnosed me with having Nyctophobia.

Throughout our countless sessions, she thinks if she cures me of that, that'll make the dreams better. That my nightmares stem from the dark. She is having a hard time understanding how horrific these dreams are.

I wonder if she is seeing a therapist.

I love going to work because I think of nothing but flowers. All my friends say I am obsessed, but who wouldn't be? It's an easy job and always smells amazing! I try to surround myself in beauty to avoid the darkness of my life—at least that's what Donna, the therapist says.

I take a quick shower, get semi ready and head to work. I love that I do not have to put a lot into my appearance for my job. It's 8 am—the perfect time because it's light outside and there are no dark areas or dark alley ways on my way.

I've planned out the perfect route to avoid any shadow spaces. You never know what is in there or lurking. The dark is dark! A shadow can be anything—an animal, a person, a box with a person inside. The list is never really ending.

Donna doesn't understand. My friends don't understand either, they don't understand why I can't just go out after 7 pm (when it gets dark) or come out for drinks (because the alcohol makes me sleepy). I just like to keep to myself and not be bothered.

Yet, I am persevering this weekend and hanging out with my oldest friend Halie. She agreed to a lunch date, daytime, perfect for her because it's a perfect time for margaritas. I haven't seen her in a while, so I am excited.

While cutting the roses, I feel pressure behind my back, like someone is pushed up against me ever so slightly. I turn around and no one is there. Typical. I feel like someone is here although it's just me in the back. It's hard for me to tell if gets colder in the room, like you read about when spirits come about, because it is always cold here.

As you can probably understand, I've grown accustomed to these daily visits. I feel like I'm partially haunted. Donna thinks this part is my overactive imagination. Imagine that. These occurrences always happen the day following one of those terrible nights.

I feel the pressure again but it's constant now. Weird, usually it's like someone brushes their body on me but this is a constant pressure, like a hug from behind. I'm frozen, the shears trembling in one hand and the rose in the other.

I'm waiting for this pressure to go away. It's not. I can't move, I feel like I can't breathe. I slowly turn my head to the right to try to check my back again, because the logical side is telling me there must be someone there now. Unfortunately, I knew before I completed the look that there was no one there. I am right.

I turn the rest of my body fast, hoping to shake that feeling like you shake a rug outside. It's gone. More than from my body, I feel it in the air, *it's* gone.

The longest I have ever stayed up before, because of these terrors, was three days. It was awful. The anxiety and irritability were no joke. The derealization was interfering with my job performance and then by the seventy-two-hour mark I was not thinking right and not paying attention. I couldn't keep track of what was happening around me, I felt like I was out of control in slow motion.

For this reason, I told myself I would never do that again. I try to get to the point of being so tired that I will, hopefully, fall asleep so deep and hard that I would not dream. My REM would not be able to function due to sleepiness. I know this is not how it works, of course, but this is what I need to tell myself to get through the day. My anxiety is through the roof as soon as the end of the day rears its ugly head because I know sleep is coming. How I wish I could. Just. Sleep.

Ding.

My phone pings its daily reminder text from Donna. *"If you get through this night, you are promised to survive all the days ahead."* Another inspirational quote from doctor google to help with my sleeping. When will she ever get that the *night* is not the big picture here?

I roll my eyes and shove my phone in my pocket and head out the door from the flower shop. Heading home, I walk a bit faster than usual because, possibly, I can out-walk the thing that was hanging out with me for the better part of the day at work. I know this is insane, but again, it makes me feel better.

I rush through the mini mart a block away from my house. I need more candles, batteries and food. I'm going to attempt an all nighter, to give my brain a break.

I fumble with my wallet, while I am frantically looking out the window to time the sunset. This cashier probably thinks I am planning to make a run for it. I pay and pull my hand away faster than he can give me change which makes the coins go everywhere. I bend down to pick them up in a rush. *Damn acrylic nails,* I think, half ready to leave the quarters where they lay.

I stand up and mumble sorry to the person behind me for taking so long, but as I turn to look at them—my heart stops. There he is… this black mass of a person!

I swing back around to the cashier, and they are not there anymore. This place is empty! I look back at this mass and try to muster anything out of my mouth. Again, it's filled with nothing but this feeling of molasses and quicksand—I can't move or make a sound.

My eyes are darting back to the window to look outside, and the sun is going down but there is still some daylight! What is happening? I try to catch my breath at the same time I close my eyes and when I breath out and open my eyes, he is gone.

The cashier is back where he was. Time stood still but I feet like I just lived a lifetime. The cashier tries to hand me my change but this time I say keep it and run out the door.

I am rushing home now. What just happened? I darted up the three flights of stairs in my apartment building, to my floor. I turn right down my hall and stop dead in my tracks. It's so fucking dark down this hall!

I immediately started crying while trying to find my phone so I could use the flashlight. My hands are shaking so bad it takes me two times to get my face recognition to work. I shoot my phone up as soon as that light is on. There is no way it should be this dark. This doesn't make sense. I can still see light outside through the three windows down the hall, but it's pitch black in here.

With my hand shaking uncontrollably, I slowly scoot my way down the hall to my apartment. Just four doors down. I am pressed against the wall, passing the first door and no signs of anything. I am swinging my light back and forth, in an attempt to flood this hall with light.

Door two. Door three and I hear a knob turn. I use the light and look at someone coming out of that first room. He is one of the regular tenants and does not seem at all bothered that there is no light. He turns around and goes down the stairs like nothing is happening. Like there is not a crazy girl here in the hall crying and terrified.

"*Hey!*" I half yell, half sob. But he does not hear me. How did he see the stairs? It's so dark. I am so close to my apartment—it does not matter.

In front of my door, I am fumbling to get my keys out. Stupid purse. My hands have not stopped shaking and it's hard for me to shine the light in my purse to find the keys. I take a deep breath, and tell myself, "Honestly Michelle, calm down." Then, three seconds after a deep breath, I jam my hand into my purse and successfully get my keys! I push the key into the keyhole faster and smoother than I ever had before.

The second I put my other hand on the knob to turn it, the hall lights turn on and flood the hallway with more light than my eyes can handle right now. I stared down the hall in disbelief. My sobs have turned into tiny hiccups of noises and sniffles.

I turn the knob and rush inside, quick to turn around and shut my door with a very intentional slam. I locked all my locks as quickly as my hands could move. I turn to lean my back against the door, a sigh of relief leaves my lungs as I close my eyes.

I open my eyes and I am in my bed. I do not remember getting in my bed. I am there, on my back, motionless. I can move my eyes only, and they are darting all around me. My room is dark, and I can see the hallway light is on. I try to move my hands, nothing. I try to yell, but I am again stopped by the heavy nothing that is in my mouth. I can't make noise, I can utter a small noise, but it's nothing. I can tell I am breathing faster, but I cannot feel my lungs move or the rise and fall of my chest. I feel nothing from my nose down. This is different. This is torture.

I hear something down the hall. Slow, sliding movements. Like when my grandpa would slowly shuffle around on carpet with his house slippers. Slow, steady, intentional. My heart is racing, at least, that's what I think it's doing. I move my eyes to the hallway light. I see nothing. No shadow but the sounds of someone walking is getting closer and closer. It sounds like the noise stops at the door. I am straining my neck to produce any whisper of a noise. I can't. That same heavy, gelatinous nothing in my throat making it impossible to make any noise.

I close my eyes in frustration and when I open them my head is hanging off the side of the bed. I was moved! Now my whole body has turned horizontal on the bed and my head is hanging over the edge! I hear those disgusting sliding footsteps but this time, by my head. Tears are streaming but going up towards my hair now.

Then I feel this... *thing*. This feeling of dread but in a ball from behind my right shoulder. Which is odd, because I am still on the bed. Like, it's coming from under the bed. Slow and steady this black, embodied, shadowed, dread of nothing-like-entity comes up from behind my shoulder and towers over me.

What is going on? I didn't go to sleep! I've been awake! I can strangle out a few crying moans but the feeling of not being able to form a word or get an actual word out is the most frustrating and terrifying thing I think I have ever experienced. This thing is looking down at me, and I see the shadow of a man. Or thing. A body.

He starts bending over with a hand outreached like he is going to grab me! Oh my God, how is this happening? My heart feels like it's going to fly out of my chest, it's thumping so loud and so fast. I half wonder If this is how a heart attack starts.

I am straining against this paralysis, to try to move

anything! I just need to move; I just need to get out of this spot. The hand is getting close. What does it want? It's heading towards... my heart? My heart!

It's reaching and I am straining. I can't move, there is no try. The closer it gets, the heavier my heart feels, the heavier my chest feels. There is nothing I can do. He is so close, that even if I do break free, it's too late.

I stop moving, I stop straining. It touches my clothes, and I close my eyes.

I take a deep breath.

Goodbye, world.

"Ashley! Ashley, get up!" Someone is shaking me awake. I shot up, drenched in sweat, I am sure I looked terrible from the look on this person's face.

"What? Why are you calling me that? What happened?" I ask. I am frantically grabbing at my chest, looking around the room, panting and sobbing. "Where am I?" I squeak out between sobs.

"Umm, Ashley...we are work. There was an accident." This is Melissa—yet, I just remember her name but do not remember how I know her.

"Wait, what? The flower shop?" I ask, panting, trying to find my breath.

Melissa looks at me like I have absolutely lost my mind. "What? What flower shop? Ashley, we are at work. At the clinic?" she says, puzzled.

"Wait, what? I don't understand..." I am so confused.

This place looks like something I dreamed of, semi-familiar but not my life.

Between my panicked sobs, Melissa tells me I hit my head and had passed out for about twenty minutes.

I get transported to the hospital where I learn my name is Ashley—not Michelle. I live in a small house with my husband and work in a medical clinic.

I do not understand what is going on. I must be dreaming. Is this the afterlife? Did I die and this is my new life or death dream? Is that a thing? What is true and what is fake?

I look for my phone and look for Donna's number. Nothing. I look for Halie's number—she will know what is going on. As I am scrolling, I don't see her name in my contacts.

I look through my text messages—nothing familiar. I have texts from people I don't know. I tap on a message from a name titled *Hubs*, and looking through the history, we have texted a long time. Silly things—things a married couple would text. There are dates from weeks, even months ago.

I click my phone off and lay back, frustrated. I don't know what's going on right now.

The doctor comes in and tells me I hit my head at work and suffered a concussion. I tell him about my real name—at least, what I think is my real name. My life at the flower shop. My cute apartment, the three flights of stairs to get there, my therapist and my friends! I tell him I had plans this weekend! I dare not bring up the demon that has been torturing me.

He states that what happened to me, in theory, is quite common—the concussion part. However, he offered no explanation of my life before. I lived a life!

As days go by, and I haven't woken up to my old life—or seen the white light—I realize I am... awake.

I am mourning my previous life, my friends, my Halie, the flower shop. Everything. I have a new therapist; his name is Ross. He tells me that there was a study of this man who was knocked on conscious before and lived a whole life. Who had no recollection of his real life when he came to, but that he is doing great now.

That's fantastic Ross, but that can't be me. There was nothing following him. I actually had this life.

I do not remember one ounce of this "real life." It's like I was dropped here in the middle of a town I've never been to or read about, given a name and told "continue your life now" ...and I am so lost!

Time goes on and I notice I no longer have this fear of sleep or my dreams—in fact, I do not dream. Now that I think about it, I haven't had a dream since then.

My husband is super confused by my actions as I am not the "same old Ashley" from before. I think he want's to leave, and frankly I don't care. I'm tired of explaining that I am not Ashley.

I am no one. I am just this entity, or this being, living but with no purpose, just aimlessly wandering this "life" with no feeling, no dreams, no friends anymore, nothing.

I am just a shell of a human.

OCtObeR

The Party

Lauren Patzer

Evelyn pushed the curled black strand of hair out of her face and examined her sexy witch outfit in the mirror. She adjusted the top to show just a little more cleavage and smiled.

"You won't be able to resist me, Justin. Not tonight," she whispered. She bit her lip naughtily and smiled at her reflection. She winked and nodded.

There was a knock on the bathroom door.

"Hey, we all gotta get ready," her roommate's voice announced.

"Sorry!" Evelyn hollered. "Come on in, I'm just about done."

Nala walked in, her bleach blonde hair a dazzling contrast to her warm brown skin. She wore a bathrobe and had a small makeup bag in her hand.

"Guess I'm not the only one looking to score tonight," Nala said and giggled.

"Justin has been single for two months now. I'm

making my move," Evelyn said as she checked her lipstick.

"Oh, you're not going after Stanley?" Nala said with a smirk.

"Seriously? What is that guy's deal?"

"He's got the crush on you bad," Nala replied. She opened up her bag as Evelyn sniffed at her.

"I'm glad this party is invite only. I can count on him not being there when I close the deal with Justin."

"Some women have a thing for nerdlings, you know."

"Not *this* woman!" Evelyn replied and walked out of the bathroom.

Two hours later, the two women walked into the suburban mini mansion on the northern outskirts of town. Nala was resplendent in her sexy nurse outfit that hugged every curve. Her long blonde hair fell gently over her shoulders in tight ringlets.

"Just a room full of Alphas," Nala whispered.

"Perfect breeding territory—just watch out for the betas!" Evelyn replied with a giggle.

Nala raised her eyebrows and approached two burly men by the fireplace. They greeted her warmly and not so subtly checked her up and down with a knowing leer.

Evelyn smiled at her friend's find and then made her way to the bar by the kitchen.

Within a few minutes, Evelyn watched as Nala walked toward the front door with both men escorting her. Her roommate glanced back at her and winked as Evelyn nodded her approval.

"She came, she saw..." Evelyn whispered enviously. She took a sip from the red cup in her hand, the cheap box wine leaving a bitter taste in her mouth as she scanned the room looking for her quarry. Soon her eyes landed on Justin, the large young man who played center for the football team dressed like a pirate. She smiled and licked her lips.

She stalked him from across the room and, just as she was about to engage him, Stanley popped his head up in her periphery.

"Hey Evie!" Stanley called. It drew everyone's attention including Justin as he glanced at Stanley closing in on Evelyn. Justin smirked.

Stanley inserted himself directly in front of Evelyn, who had to stop to avoid running the lanky youth down. She stopped and looked at him with a sigh. His ever present glasses matched the simple lab coat he wore with a pocket protector in the pocket.

"Oh, Doctor Stanley, I presume?" Evelyn said in a sweet mocking voice. If Stanley detected any sourness in her voice, he didn't show it. He just smiled a big grin.

"You look great!" He gushed. "Can I get you a drink?"

Evelyn looked down at the drink in her hand with a frown. Then a thought struck her.

"Oh, sure!" She said with a smile. "Can you get me a seven and seven?"

"You bet!" Stanley replied and took off with a surprising quickness toward the bar.

At least he's enthusiastic, Evelyn thought as her eyes

returned to Justin and the smile dropped from her face. Julie, the sorority President was decked out in a slutty angel costume that barely covered any of her lily white flesh and pulled Justin's eyes toward her bountiful cleavage.

"Fuck," Evelyn cursed. She turned to see where Stanley had run off to and collided with a large man pushing seven feet tall wearing a hockey mask and tattered clothing. Evelyn gently pushed herself back from him and felt his thick chest muscles under her fingers for a moment.

"Well, aren't you a big boy?" Evelyn asked as she brought her cup to her lips.

The man grunted and turned around, heading away from her. Evelyn sighed.

Stanley returned with her drink. She accepted it graciously.

"Any snacks? Looks like I'll be going hungry tonight," she quipped.

"Oh sure, let me go find some!" Stanley beamed and ran off again. Evelyn shook her head.

She wandered through the house toward a hallway and was just finishing her second drink when she heard the screams coming from the living room behind her. Stanley came tearing toward her and grabbed her hand. He pulled her into a closet and shut the door. He locked the handle. Evelyn rolled her eyes in the darkness.

"Really, Stanley, I don't think—" she began to say but Stanley pushed his fingers against her lips and shushed her. As her eyes adjusted to the darkness, there was just enough light streaming in through the bottom of the door for her to see his eyes staring at the closed door. There were more screams and crashing outside the door far away, but getting closer.

Voices plead for mercy, and then went silent with a crack and a thud. Suddenly, the closet door handle jiggled and Evelyn's eyes went wide.

"Hey, what the fuck?" a man's voice called from down the hallway. There was the sound of feet running toward the closet. A man yelled and then, with a sickening thud, he hit the floor in front of the closet. Evelyn watched the shadows moving under the crack beneath the door. Then, with a boom, a head came through the thin door, busting a hole in it. Blood dripped down the inside of the door as Evelyn and Stanley tried to shrink into the shadows.

The head dropped from the door as the body hit the ground again. The light thru the gap disappeared as an eye peered inside, hidden behind a hockey mask.

"Oh my God!" a voice screamed from behind the head peering through and the mask disappeared from the hole in the door. They listened as more screams cried out from further away. Stanley grabbed the door handle and opened the door. It opened just a smidge before colliding with a prone dead or unconscious form on the floor. They both pushed and got the door to open just enough for them to squeeze out.

Justin lay on the floor just outside the closet, his face bloodied and his lifeless eye staring up at the ceiling. His head lay in a puddle of shredded brain matter and blood.

"Justin, no," Evelyn whispered as Stanley pulled her away. Her stomach rumbled angrily.

Stanley dragged Evelyn to a back door and they ran from the house.

Evelyn allowed Stanley to lead her down the street to an abandoned house. He pulled her through the door, and then closed and locked it behind him.

"That was horrible," Evelyn whispered as she leaned against the wall, her face lit by the moonlight streaming in through a window.

"Yeah," Stanley agreed. "But on the bright side, now all those dudes are gone, so I have you all to myself."

"Wha… what?" Evelyn asked, her voice shaking.

"Don't worry. That big guy is my brother. He's a little unstable, but he'll do anything I ask him to. Now with all those other guys out of the picture, you won't be distracted anymore. We can finally be together." Stanley stepped closer to Evelyn, but she stepped back into the shadows.

"You killed them all? For me?" Evelyn asked, her voice shook and quivered. Her stomach rumbled again.

"I would do anything for you!" Stanley exclaimed.

"Well," Evelyn replied her voice a bit raspier than before accompanied by the sound of clothes rustling. "I really underestimated you, Stanley."

"I am full of surprises," Stanley said with a confident smile.

"Oh, so am I," Evelyn replied before she stepped

forward back into the moonlight. Her head had transformed into a slick black mound with eight glistening, ebony eyes that twinkled in the low light. Her mouth was now a set of jagged mandibles that dripped with saliva.

"No!" Stanley screamed, stepping back against the wall. He held up his arms to fend her off. "What are you?"

"Just what you wanted, Stanley. The perfect mate!" Evelyn screeched as she used four of her eight hairy limbs to pin Stanley against the wall. Her stinger flashed forth but just lightly grazed his chest, ripping through the fabric and scraping along his skin leaving the barest scratch. Little beads of blood formed along the scratch as the tiniest bit of her venom penetrated into his bloodstream. The exotic substance slowed him down, but didn't totally immobilize him. She spun him around multiple times, wrapping his upper torso with a thin but incredibly strong, sticky webbing before she secured him to the wall, facing her.

"What was your brother's name again?" Evelyn hissed as she brought her face closer to Stanley's watering eyes.

"Chris! Chris! Help me!" Stanley shouted.

"Chris?" Evelyn asked. "Is that short for Christopher?"

"Chris! Please, help me!" Stanley shouted and began sobbing.

Evelyn scuttled silently to the door and unlocked it, cracking it open before she disappeared back into the shadows.

"Chris!" Stanley shouted again, but this time a grunt answered him from just outside the building before the hulking killer crashed through the door. He looked at Stanley and ripped off his mask, revealing a scarred visage that looked burned by acid.

"Such a delicious specimen," Evelyn whispered from somewhere in the dark corners of the room.

"Watch out!" Stanley shouted.

Chris turned and rushed into the darkness; a large machete glistening with the blood of the night's victims raised high. He stopped cold after only going a few feet, his limbs held fast by a thick sticky rope invisible in the inky abyss. Writhing wildly, the large man attempted to free himself but only connected with additional strands of the web until he could barely move at all.

Evelyn appeared in her spider form and raised her head up so it was even with Chris', exposing a large red hourglass on her abdomen. She plucked one strand with her foot and Chris growled.

"Predator and prey," she whispered to him in a husky rasp. "How does it feel?"

"Please!" Stanley shouted. "Don't hurt him! He was only following my orders."

"Oh," Evelyn replied. "I wish I could do that but, you see, I'm not like my sister Nala. She prefers to completely paralyze her victims before she consumes them. I think that's terribly boring and much too humane, especially for little beasts like you two. No, I give my dinner just a taste of venom to make them easier to handle while I consume them bit by bit. They are fully aware and can feel exactly what's happening to them. The fear in their eyes is like a dessert topping. Their cries and whimpers of despair are an enticing spice."

Evelyn tapped her stinger into Chris' abdomen slightly as he jerked in pain. He growled again, his heavily scarred face contorted.

"So strong," Evelyn whispered huskily. "Many of them are before I start."

Evelyn laughed and the eerie sound echoed off the walls accompanied by the rhythmic clattering of her mandibles.

"Please," Stanley whimpered. "He doesn't understand he did anything wrong. He's innocent."

"Now, Stanley," Evelyn replied. "You shouldn't use an expendable tool if you're not prepared to lose it."

She moved to Chris' left hand, held fast by the webbing.

"Let's see how long you can go without screaming, big guy," Evelyn said. Her razor sharp mandibles clipped the end of his pinky finger and the big man growled. She bit off the end of the tender pink tip of his pinky and he cried out before growling again. Blood spurted briefly from the tip before it settled down into the small drip.

"Well," Evelyn murmured. "That wasn't long at all."

Her mandibles dug into the flesh of his pinky finger, breaking through the tiny bone there with an audible crunch. Chris groaned shrilly as he clenched his jaw.

Evelyn made quick work of the entire pinky finger,

gobbling down the flesh, blood and bone as she went. Chris broke and screamed.

"There we go," Evelyn congratulated him. "That's a proper reaction."

Chris's muscles strained as he tried to break free of the webbing that held him in place.

"Oh darling, I've held bigger men than you in place with less, but I do appreciate the struggle. Makes it more exciting for me."

She moved onto to the rest of Chris' fingers as Stanley sobbed across the room. She stepped back from her handiwork as blood dripped from the stubby knuckles where the fingers had been.

"Oh, but I forget my manners," Evelyn said as she stepped to Chris's right hand and snipped the large blade free from the webbing and, of course, Chris other fingers. It dropped to the ground and Evelyn transformed back into the woman Stanley had run into the room with. She stood naked in front of Chris as she picked the machete up from the floor.

"I think it's only fair you feel the bite of this blade, so you can truly appreciate the work you did earlier tonight," she said as she raised the blade into the air. She stopped and looked at Stanley.

"Don't you think he did a good job tonight, Stanley? I really believe he did everything you asked him to."

"Please," Stanley whimpered.

"You were so brave earlier, Stanley. I'm a little

disappointed." She said and swung the blade down into Chris' left shoulder. Blood spurted into the air splashing Evelyn's naked human form as Chris threw his head back and howled. She laughed and dropped the blade.

"You bitch!" Stanley erupted. He struggled against his bonds, his crimson face contorted with rage. He picked his feet up and pressed them against the wall behind him, but the super adhesive properties of his bonds kept him in place.

"There's the little psychopath," Evelyn said. "The tears weren't very convincing. Unfortunately, I'm afraid you won't be perfecting your technique."

She raised her hand to Chris' cheek and caressed it. He tried to bite her. She pulled her hand away as she giggled. She reached back to his face and tapped his nose.

"Feisty!"

She put her face close to Chris as her face bubbled and transformed, her head swelling to consume nearly all her hair with just bits poking through the slick ebon skull. Her human eyes disappeared, to be replaced by eight dark orbs shining in the moonlight.

"And delicious!" She hissed. She went back to his left hand and consumed the bleeding flesh, ripping bits off with the mandibles quickly, bone and flesh disappearing in a whirl of activity. Chris screamed as the damage was done, while Stanley struggled in vain to free himself.

Evelyn stopped when she completed consuming Chris' hand. She patched the stub with a bit of webbing to staunch the blood flow, then moved to his other hand and quickly made work of it too. She patched it as well and then dropped to the ground. Her mandibles sliced through the leather work boots and socks and peeled them away before she repeated the consumption process with his feet, patching them up as well.

The big man's head hung forward as he gasped and whimpered. Evelyn placed a smooth claw under his chin and raised his face up to hers.

"But I think it's only fair that you get to see you were successful tonight. Stanley is going to get lucky."

Evelyn snipped the thick strands holding Chris in place and expertly whirled him around so he faced his brother across the room. She transformed back into a naked human, her skin still wet with Chris's blood. She turned to face Stanley and walked to him, swinging her hips and drawing her fingers across the blood on her chest.

"This is what you wanted, wasn't it, Stanley?"

"What the hell?!" Stanley screamed.

She dropped to her knees and grabbed Stanley's legs as he tried to kick her.

"Aww, I thought you'd be more excited to see me naked," Evelyn said with a pout.

She transformed back into her arachnid form and quickly pulled Stanley's clothes off his lower half. His limp manhood stared back at her.

"Well, this won't do at all," she said and reverted to human form. She manipulated his genitals with one hand while she caressed his face with the other. Glands beneath her arms exuded a pheromone that made Stanley shudder. Despite his conscious thought, the powerful chemicals dragged his subconscious into a haze of lust and frenzy. His eyes only caught brief glimpses of Evelyn's face as she mounted him. He felt a curious wet and warm tugging at his crotch as stroke after stroke he grunted with more intensity. His eyes glazed over as he erupted and his mind wavered between seeing Evelyn's human face and the arachnid one she'd horrified him with before, but he didn't care and lost himself in wild abandon.

The arachnid form of Evelyn stepped back from the wheezing Stanley, still suspended on the wall. She tapped the red hourglass on her abdomen and nodded.

"That should do nicely," she said. She looked at Stanley and sighed. "I'm always so hungry after doing it."

She lunged forward with her mandibles and snapped them with a crunch through Stanley's neck. His head fell to the floor as blood gushed like a burbling fountain from his neck. Behind her, Chris screamed in agony.

She turned to Chris.

"I'll be back to you soon. This is Stanley's moment," she said.

She retrieved Stanley's head and quickly crunched through his face and skull as she consumed everything including the brain matter, which was a delectable treat. Chris sobbed as she consumed the rest of Stanley.

She turned to the crying hulk and tittered.

"Don't despair, Chris. Your flesh will help grow a whole new generation of my children."

He screamed at her and then screamed in agony as she finished consuming first his arms and then his legs. She quickly finished the rest of him as he'd gone into shock and was no longer conscious.

When she was done, she retrieved her webbing and rolled it into a little ball she held with one claw. She retrieved her human clothing with the other and disappeared into the night.

An hour later, she crawled in through her upper floor apartment window. She transformed back into her human form as she set her clothes on the floor. Nala stepped out of the bathroom in a towel freshly showered and looked at Evelyn standing naked before her, tan skin streaked with her victims' blood.

"Huh," Nala replied. "So we both got lucky tonight?"

Evelyn grinned.

"You done in the bathroom?" Evelyn asked.

Nala laughed and nodded.

November

Ghostly Soldiers
Daniel DiQuinzio

1.

It was the night of the first Friday of November. The year was 1976. As the alarm clock on the bedside table ticked away, Helena Arturo slept beside her husband, Peter. As midnight approached, Helena heard a strange and loud noise coming from outside the house that woke her. She sat up and listened to the noise, realizing that it was music. There was something both very unnatural and unearthly to it that terrified her. In addition, Helena realized this music was coming from somewhere very close to their house in the Kenningston neighborhood of Philadelphia. That fact horrified Helena and she was not even sure why.

On instinct, she sought her husband's protection. Her hand reached over to her husband's shoulder. She shook it. Peter woke and looked at his wife. "Is something wrong, my dear?" he asked.

"I am not certain, Peter," Helena replied. "I thought I

heard *music….* but now I hear nothing.”

"I don't hear anything, Helena.”

"I *know* I heard music.”

"I believe you, my darling.” Peter leaned over, kissing his wife's cheek. "Perhaps you're just worried about Alberto and Sarah visiting on Monday as the newspapers say it is supposed to rain that night.”

"Maybe you are right, Peter.”

"You should go back to sleep, Helena. Everything will be all right.”

"In a few minutes, Peter. I want to stretch my legs first and shake off this eerie feeling. I'll be back soon.”

Helena kissed her husband then slipped out from underneath the bed sheets. She pulled her robe on over her nightgown and walked down the hall toward the bathroom. Helen and Peter owned their own row house. This style of home was built in a connected row where each house shared a wall between them. Could this be the explanation for the unusual sound?

Helena started to hear the music again as she walked. It was much louder now, seeming even closer to them. It was so late at night that the noise was even more peculiar. Helena's thoughts turned to their four children. She and Peter had raised two sons and two daughters. They were all grown now but they all regularly visited their parents.

As she approached the bathroom, the music slipped away again and Helena only heard the creaking of the pipes. However, after a moment, the music returned. Even louder this time. Helena was baffled. What was the cause? She listened closer and ascertained drum beats? Yes. Rhythmic, deep drums.

Helena entered the bathroom. Through the window, she observed a most unusual group of figures who were very curiously proceeding along the sidewalk, which made her wonder why they would be out for a walk at this late hour. Could she discern more about these figures if she watched them? She could. Following a few minutes, all she succeeded in deducing was that they all wore the same style of clothing and that all of them carried some long object in their hands. Was it possible to learn more if she got closer? Helena moved over to the window and then her face turned pale white in shock because her eyes saw through these individuals. How was that possible? They were translucent.

She stood there and tracked the movements of these unknown people. Once again, she heard the deep rhythmic, beating of drums. Was this what woke her? It was. Where was it coming from? She did not know.

Helena was startled when she heard the bathroom clock chime the hour of midnight. The music vanished. As she stood there, Helena discovered all the figures she previously observed were gone from the sidewalk.

2.

One night later, Helena stood bent over the living room couch as she and her husband set up the mattress within it. Alberto, their oldest son, and his wife, Sarah, would be sleeping on it, as Alberto was attending a weeklong historical conference in the city.

Helena froze, hearing an instrumental refrain coming from outside their home. What was it? Drums being played. Was it the rhythmic beat from last night? It was.

Helena's body became rigid in alarm as she focused herself on the rhythmic vibrations and she struggled to breath while her lungs puffed in anxiety. Peter sensed something was amiss with his wife and so he looked at her filled with worry. "What's wrong Helena?" he asked.

"I hear... drum beats, Peter," Helena whispered. "Peter, do you hear drum beats coming from outside?"

"I do," he chuckled. "It's nothing to worry about. Come on, we've got work to do."

Helena heard the melody increase sharply, which was accompanied by a great uptake in its intensity because as she and Peter pulled the mattress out onto the carpet. Her heart pounded in terror as the rhythm neared their home. Why did it frighten her so? She remembered the strange characters she witnessed last night whose bodies appeared to be immaterial and the mere memory made her shed tears of distress while her lips rapidly moved in angst. Was there a connection between them and the drumbeats? It was possible. Did she want to know what the connection was? She did not. Helena chose to forget about those spectral beings.

Over her rapid heartbeat, Helena heard the small clock, which rested on the table beside the soda, toll midnight. It frightened her. The music ceased making her heart rate slow to its normal beat as her emotions stabilized. It was only then she knew her husband was staring at her with a grave look of concern on his chiseled face. "Helena, what's wrong?" he inquired.

"The music I heard is gone," Helena stuttered. "I don't want to know what caused it."

Peter stroked his wife's cheeks reassuring her that she was safe. Helena's lips ceased their erratic movement in the seconds it took him to wipe away the tears. She kissed his lips in gratitude. "You are exhausted, Helena," Peter stated. "You should sleep."

"Alberto and Sarah will be here tomorrow," Helena objected. "I need to make up the mattress."

"That can be done tomorrow afternoon. Right now, you need to rest."

Peter slid his arm around Helena's waist pulling her close to him. He walked forward. Helena did not protest as he led her to their bedroom, for after enduring the return of those terrifying beating of drums, she felt relieved.

3.

The rain was torrential on Sunday night. Alberto Arturo struggled to make out the street as he drove the station wagon to his parents' home. He and his wife endured this storm for much of their trip to Philadelphia. As he stared ahead, Alberto's lower right leg, which was a rubber leg, ached as it always did in such terrible weather ever since he lost the real one at the end of his service in the Vietnam War as an officer in the United States Marine Corps to a landmine. A few groans came from his lips but he tightened his grip on the steering wheel as he was determined to fight through this agonizing pain to accomplish his task.

Those sounds alarmed Sarah, who sat in the passenger seat, not just as Alberto's wife but also as a nurse in the United States Navy. It was through her medical capacity the two first met, because Sarah was one of the nurses assigned to Alberto's ward in the naval hospital he briefly resided in following his return from Vietnam. The two of them fell in love during his recovery and they married shortly after the Marine Corps gave Alberto a medical discharge. "Alberto, it's not wise for you to continue driving in your present condition," Sarah stated. "You'll need to pull over so we can change off."

"I'll manage," Alberto replied. "I've gotten used to this pain over the years."

"I will not take no for an answer. It's a violation of my

medical ethics to allow you to continue driving in this condition."

"It doesn't matter, my parent's home is dead ahead," Alberto grunted. "My beloved Mrs. Arturo, we're at the end of our journey."

Sarah smiled. It always seemed magical when her husband called her by her married name. Her birth name was Sarah Chang, and after their marriage, Sarah took her husband's last name as her own. She was an old-fashioned Catholic woman and loved thinking of herself as being Mrs. Alberto Arturo.

Through the rain she and her husband noticed a bright light shining out from the front of the Arturo's home, which acted as a beacon guiding their station wagon safely into the driveway. Alberto shifted into park and honked the horn signaling their arrival to his parents. "Come on, Sarah," he called. "Once more into the breach."

"I'm right behind you," Sarah replied. "Thankfully soon we will be warm and dry."

Helena face was awash with worry while she watched the storm through the living room window. At this moment, she prayed for the safety of her son and daughter-in-law who were passing through it on the way from their apartment in Newark, New Jersey. Her heart pulsed in excitement, after she heard a horn honk. "Peter," she squealed. "Sarah and Alberto are here."

"Stay here where it's dry," Peter instructed. "I'll go

out and help them.”

"Stay safe, my dear.”

"I intend to.”

Outside, Alberto and Sarah trekked bravely over the wet grass to the front door while the rain laid siege to them. As he kept pace beside her, Sarah heard her continued murmurs from the man she loved, which worried her greatly. Although she knew he would never admit it, Sarah feared the rain doused her husband's prosthetic limb causing it to swell and through that resulted in the severe anguish he must be experiencing at this very moment. Soon they reached the bottom of the steps. Sarah looked fixedly ahead and smiled seeing her father-in-law waiting there for them.

"It looks as if you've both taken your shower already,” Peter joked. "Now I don't think either of you need one.”

"Hello, Mister Arturo,” Sarah replied. "It's good to see you.”

"Give me your bags you two and I'll bring them inside.”

Sarah handed her duffel bag to her father-in-law. Alberto did the same. Peter made an about face, meaning he turned around, and he ported the bags up and through the front door while the two arrivals followed him. As he crossed the threshold into his home, Alberto groaned for a second time from the discomfort caused by his enlarged prosthetic limb.

Helena Arturo was in a deep state of unease as she brought a tray on top of which, sat several cups of hot tea to the front door. The cause was the horrific musical beat she endured listening to for the last two nights. She could still hear the unearthly tune repeating itself in her mind, which made her heart pound in terror at the memory. On this night, she dreaded the possible return of this strange and otherworldly beating of drums.

From outside the row home Helena heard something. She abruptly stopped. Her bright pink lips quivered and her fingers trembled, which were all indicators she was possessed by a deep and abiding terror that the dreaded tones return to resume its gruesome work. She wobbled in her high heels. Helena's eyes darted to and from seeking to triangulate where the audio disruption came from while she stood there struggling to hold the tray still. As she shivered, Helena forced herself to listen to this noise. What did she hear? Something hitting the row home. What was it? It was only rain.

Helena took several deep breaths to steady her nerves. Her eyes glanced at the silver wedding ring on her finger, which reminded her she was still the lady of this row home. With that title came certain duties she must perform. One of them was being the dutiful hostess for her and Peter's guests, even when she did not feel up to the task. Helena practiced smiling several times, which enabled her to cloak her fears behind an image of happiness and as soon as she appeared to be once again composed, Helena resumed her forward movement. She continued her course.

While her high heels clicked together, she found her mind still dwelled on the recurrent music, which she feared would continue to haunt her. Where did it come from? That was unknown. Was it gone for good? She hoped it was. Would it return tonight? She feared it would. Would it continue beyond tonight? She feared that most of all.

Helena knew as she moved over the carpet she must not display her trepidation under any circumstances to any one in her family. Soon, she came to the front door. Helena saw her husband standing in front of it with Alberto and Sarah while their soaked clothes dripped on the carpet. They discarded their jackets and their shoes to dry. Helena walked around the luggage, which sat on the carpet, to offer the tray of tea to her family members and all the while continued to dutifully smile concealing behind it her profound trepidation that she was trapped within an endless nightmare from, which she would never wake.

"Hello Alberto, welcome home," she chirped. "Hello Sarah, I'm sorry you were caught in this storm."

"It's all right Mother, I endured worse rain in the jungles of Vietnam," Alberto interjected. "To me this storm is a mere mild spring rain."

"That's nothing, you should've seen the rain my old regiment endured in the North African and the Sicilian campaigns during the Second World War," Peter chortled. "Compared to that both this storm and the rain in Vietnam are nothing but annoyances."

Sarah and Helena both smiled and pretended to enjoy the war stories that their respective husbands told but in truth, they were both annoyed. Peter took the cup of tea that was closest to him. "Thank you, my darling," he addressed his wife. "I'm going to shower and change."

"Yes dear," Helena replied. "I'll keep our guests company."

Peter went upstairs to the bathroom leaving Helena downstairs with Alberto and Sarah who drank the other two cups of tea. As she watched them, a shiver spread across her body in response to a sound, which she detected vibrating through the walls. At first, she feared it was the unnatural symphony returning to continue its work. Helena's fingers became tense knowing she could not allow Alberto and Sarah to see the great state of terror in which she existed on this night and so she forced herself to not panic while she monitored the noise. Her emotions calmed once she knew it was just water rushing through the pipes.

Soon, Helena's state of anxiety ended but the sounds that disturbed her were still coming through the walls. She continued smiling. In a few minutes, Alberto and Sarah were finished drinking their tea and both returned their cups to the tray, which made Helena remember there was another task she needed to carry out. "Alberto, I've made a place for you and Sarah to sleep," she reported. "You'll be using the mattress in the living room. I'm sure you'll both like it."

"Oh we'll definitely enjoy it, Mrs. Arturo," Sarah

agreed. "It'll be very romantic sleeping in such tight confines with my husband."

"You two should shower first. I'll have Peter bring your luggage to your living room for you."

Alberto snaked his right arm under Sarah's left arm securely fastening her to him. He advanced forward. "Come, my dear. We'll shower together."

"Yes, my husband," Sarah agreed excitedly. "That sounds very romantic indeed."

4.

This is the last trip," Peter muttered. "After this, I'm done."

Helena accompanied her husband. "I knew this wouldn't take long," she teased. "Especially not for such a strong man as yourself, Peter."

"Strength has nothing to do with this, Helena. My first job after high school was working as a hotel porter."

Peter entered the living room carrying the last of his guest's luggage and grunted putting the bag on the floor beside the other pieces of baggage. Helena stopped next to him. She breathed heavily worrying that tonight she would continue hearing the ghastly loud drum beats that disturbed her for two consecutive nights.

Outside, the storm intensified. Helena felt her heart beat rapidly when she detected something that was louder than the storm and it was possible her nightmare resumed but it was only a brief second before she calmed down after remembering the noise was only the pipes creaking. Tears began to form within her eyes. It dawned upon her that she now existed in a constant state of terror about the return of the ghastly loud drum beats.

"That's done," Peter groaned. "Our guests are all set for the night."

"I'm glad Peter," Helena cried. "We'll be able to get out of here soon."

Peter whirled around. Through keen observation, he noticed the clear signs of emotional distress on his wife's face. He ran his fingers along her cheeks comforting her by stroking them. "I've... been thinking and pondering... the music I heard," Helena stammered. "Do you think I should tell our guests?

"I wouldn't," Peter answered. "Even if it returned, I doubt it could be heard through the storm."

"Oh, I hope you're right Peter," Helena sobbed. "Oh Peter... I just don't want to hear this music ever again."

5.

Alberto moved very awkwardly alongside his wife, which was due to his rubber limb having swollen up on him as they were on the way to the living room to change out of their wet clothes. From his lips came murmurs of agony. They aroused Sarah's deep concern prompting her to extend her arm out to him. "Lean on me Alberto," she ordered. "I'll carry you if your rubber leg hurts too much for you to walk."

"It's only stiff," Alberto responded. "This always happens on a night such as this."

"I fear it is more than that."

"I can manage."

On their brief trip, Alberto followed his Marine Corps training by focusing his mind on something else to distract himself from the anguish he felt. In this case, it was the conference he was attending this week at Independence Hall. Its purpose was to celebrate the bicentennial anniversary of the signing of the Declaration of Independence. On the conference's first day, Alberto would be delivering a paper that was influenced by both the British Bill of Rights and the Virginia Declaration of Rights upon Thomas Jefferson's drafting of the Declaration of Independence. He peered ahead with his dark black eyes and determined they were approaching their destination. In only a few seconds, he could end his momentary suffering by removing his rubber limb again and this time set it aside to dry.

Alberto and Sarah entered the living room finding Peter and Helena waiting for them. Helena looked at the young couple. Unknown to them she was worried her façade would crack in their presence, exposing all of her fears to them before she could escape to the sanctuary of her bedroom. "Let me know if you'll need anything else," she informed her guests.

"Thank you mother," Alberto replied. "Right now all we need is some privacy."

Peter wrapped his hand around Helena's palm. "Come on, my dear," he told her. "We'll prepare dinner as they change."

6.

Several hours later, Sarah and Alberto lay in their improvised sleeping accommodations reading while Alberto's prosthetic limb dried out against the wall. Outside, the storm reached its climax. While she read her romance novel, Sarah's ears detected something coming from outside, which aroused her curiosity. To her surprise, it sounded as if someone outside the building was playing musical instruments. As she paid attention to it, Sarah gasped and dropped her novel on the floor in alarm. In response, Albert set aside his history book and focused his bearing upon his wife. "Sarah, what's wrong?" he inquired.

"I... heard music being played outside," Sarah responded. "I think it's drum beats."

Alberto noted his wife's unease. In accordance with his Marine training, he monitored the night with his ears but at first, he could only make out raindrops. Soon afterwards, he heard something over the storm. "I hear it also," he reported. "You're right—it's drum beats."

Although, Sarah felt very reassured to learn the existence of these instruments was not something she imagined but she made no response because her mind was preoccupied assessing the actions produced by the chords. Their volume increased by several decimals. That indicated to her it was approaching the row home and prompted her to decide to leave the mattress. "I'll return shortly," she muttered, adding, "I need to investigate something. It's this music... I need to investigate it further."

Sarah slid out from underneath the sheets. Alberto watched his wife ambulate in her red satin nightgown to the living room window to spy on what was occurring outside the home. There, Sarah stopped. She pulled on the cord making the window shade rise up, revealing the sidewalk. "Alberto!" Sarah screamed. "Come here at once, you need to see this!"

Alberto left the mattress. He hobbled over to his wife on his one intact leg while he continued to pay attention to the eerie pounding discerning it was becoming clearer to understand. On some level, Alberto was certain the timing of their appearance was vaguely recognizable. He halted beside his wife and saw Sarah was frozen solid in a state of sheer terror. "What's wrong, my dear?" he asked.

"Those peculiar tunes," Sarah answered. "They're coming from... the sidewalk. Just look out the window Alberto... and you'll see."

In the master bedroom, Helena Arturo jolted awake in response to a loud clanging and banging coming through the bedroom window. She attentively monitored these audio disturbances as they continued, soon glimpsing that it was more than a mere set of noises but was an instrumental arrangement that sounded alarmingly familiar. The reason hit her. Helena sat up in a cold sweet and struggled to accept the reality that the drumming, which stalked her at night returned, as she dreaded would happen. The time, she needed to know the time. That was the only way to determine if what she feared actually occurred and as such she leaned over to study the clock sitting on the bedside table. Her heart sank. It was now almost midnight, which made Helena's eyes release tears of great sadness in response to the continuation of her torment.

Acting solely upon instinct, Helena reached over gripping her husband's shoulder and shook it. "Peter, wake up," she screamed. "Oh please…. Please, I need you to wake up."

Peter's eyes opened in response to his wife's desperate pleas. He sat up beside her. At once, he began stroking Helena's long blonde hair in a desperate attempt to calm her down. "What's wrong, Helena?" he asked.

"That music… Peter!" she cried. "Oh, Peter, it's as I feared, that dreadful music is back."

Helena's tears continued. In this dark twilight hour she doubted even her husband to whom she always looked to be her great protector could save her from the great escalating terrors which were arising within her. Peter pulled her close to him. She rested her weary head on his broad shoulder and rested it there while he continued rubbing her hair. Although Helena's tears continued, she felt reassured by his presence. "Oh Peter," she cried. "I'm deathly afraid of that music and I don't want... to hear it *ever* again... I can't bear to ever hear it again."

"Then you won't, Helena," Peter whispered. "I've got a plan. We'll implement it tomorrow."

7.

In the Arturo's living room, Alberto and Sarah found themselves in front of the window with their eyes peering out into the stormy November night bearing witness to a group of very strange men that moved down the sidewalk. They could only be seen because of the glowing streetlamps. All Sarah and Alberto could infer about the group they studied was that it was a collection of men dressed in archaic clothes and all of their hands were clasped around some long object and that they were proceeding in unison down the sidewalk organized into columns of two. Two figures at the front carried a large fluttering cloth. Rain dripped down them. Sarah was unnerved that the tune, which led to this discovery, was still increasing in volume.

As the strangers came closer to the Arturo row home, Sarah thought she saw raindrops pass through their forms. She knew that could not occur. As a trained nurse, Sarah believed there must be a more logical and scientific explanation for it inspiring her medically trained mind to conclude it could only have been a trick of the light which occurred from the street lamps shining down on these men. "Alberto, those figures... who are they?" she inquired.

"I don't know, Sarah," Alberto responded. "I don't know."

The marching men were close enough to the window now that Sarah and Alberto could see their appearance in detail, freezing them a trance of great terror because on each of these figures their skin and eyes were devoid of color. Sarah wanted to shout. She fought the urge to do so as she felt such an action would be unbecoming of a nurse or any other officer in the United States. That did not prevent her eyes from peering through all these creatures because they along with their clothes and the objects they all carried were immaterial.

Sarah's lips and her eyes widened as a primal sense of fear consumed her, breaking through all of her discipline as a Naval officer, shaking her to the core of her being. At once, the instincts passed down to her through the generations of women who came before her took hold of her and she screamed out in terror seeking the protection that only her husband could provide to her. "Alberto, it can't be possible... It isn't possible!" she cried. "Honey, did you... see what I saw?"

"I did, my love," Alberto responded. "I saw it also."

"It can't be true and they can't be real."

"I'm afraid both are so Sarah."

"What're they?"

"I have no explanation, Sarah, but I fear we're

witnessing ghosts."

"We both believe in the lingering presence of spirits but there must be a more logical explanation."

"I'm afraid it's true, Sarah. I wish I knew how this was possible. But I don't, all I know is they're ghosts."

"Ghosts of whom?"

"I don't know."

Alberto studied the appearance of these figures. Soon he came to know each man among this group was dressed in what appeared to be the outlines of a jacket with something resembling a shirt underneath it. On their head was a round hat. As a military man, he understood this outfit resembled a military uniform and he also suspected the reason why all of these figures were moving in unison. He found the strength of will to force him to gaze closer at the figures at the front. They were flag bearers. Alberto was taken aback at the designs of the images on the cloth, which confirmed Alberto's suspicions. "What are they wearing, Alberto?" Sarah inquired of her husband.

"Uniforms, Sarah," Alberto responded. "Those are the uniforms of Continental Soldiers they're wearing."

"It can't be so, that's impossible."

"It may be impossible, but it's still the truth, Sarah."

"What're they doing?"

"Marching, somehow these ghosts are marching in formation."

"Why've they come here?"

"I've got no answers for that question at this time."

"What're they doing on this street at this hour?"

"I don't know, Sarah."

Alberto and Sarah continued to watch the Continental soldiers as they approached the Arturo's row house. Then Sarah saw something else in the distance making her fight through her fear to point her finger at the window "Look, Alberto," Sarah stuttered. "There are more people coming towards us... behind these figures."

Coming into view was a second small band of immaterial men who were able to somehow hold see through versions of musical instruments and were following the marching soldiers down the sidewalk. It was organized into columns of two. At the front were two men who were busy pounding their sticks on the cloth drums and following them were two men who were busy making bugle calls. Behind them two musicians played trumpets. At the rear were two men playing their pipes.

"What's the other group of figures supposed to be Alberto?" Sarah asked.

"They must be Continental Minstrels."

"Why's that?"

"During the Revolutionary War, minstrels were part of the Continental Army, they would accompany the troops and play their instruments as the troops marched into battle against the British soldiers. All of these beings must all be ghosts of Continental soldiers."

"That can't be so Alberto, the dead can't walk and they can't play music."

"I'm afraid it must be so Sarah. The time—" he gasped, "—what's the time?!"

"It's almost midnight."

"Music coming from outside," Alberto muttered. "Music is being played outside when it's close to midnight."

Alberto went silent. The timing of the manifestation of the eerie symphony made him certain someone once informed him of a similar phenomenon a long time ago but he could not recall when this occurred or who it was who informed him of it. He continued to watch the two groups of ghostly Continental troops with his wife as they continued forward keeping pace with the music. To the great surprise of Alberto and Sarah all of these ghostly images made a right face, a right turn, and moved down the path leading to the Arturo row house. Sarah felt her anxiousness increase before her very eyes as the ghosts reached the front steps. She forced herself to speak. "Why are those figures coming this way Alberto?" Sarah asked.

"I don't know my dear," Alberto replied. "I truly don't know."

The figures did not stop. Sarah and Alberto watched through the rain as all of them ascended the front steps, which occurred while the orchestration's volume increased significantly before all of them halted. Then all of the soldiers made an about face, which meant they all turned around at once, and now they faced towards the street, as the flag bearers and the instrument bearers behind them did the same reversing the order of the formation. The minstrels moved away from the Arturo residence.

Sarah and Alberto stood still on the floor of the Arturo's living room as they watched long dead members of the Continental Army head down the front steps. Sarah tracked them with her eyes knowing her husband was doing the same. Soon all of these ghostly regulars made a left face, a left turn, onto the sidewalk. The pace of the instruments was becoming more rapid than ever before while the musicians led their companions to the corner. There they halted. Behind them, the soldiers and the flag bearers followed their example.

The music came to its loud finale. As Sarah and Alberto stood there waiting in terrible anticipation to discover what horrific feat these apparitions would do next, when to their amazement the minstrels disappeared from sight. The tune was still audible. Seconds later, the soldiers evaporated. The musical leaders of their small brigade followed suit but the music continued to linger before it finally vanished leaving only a rain soaked sidewalk.

Sarah still doubted that these vanished men were ghosts and sought the advice and counsel of her husband. "Those figures can't have been reenactors," she muttered. "They can't have been soldiers from the Revolutionary War as otherwise they would all be dead by now." She looked up at her husband. "Who're they? What are they, my love?"

"There's only one logical possibility," Alberto responded. "They must've all been the ghosts of Continental soldiers who served in the Pennsylvania line."

"Why are they moving on the sidewalk?"

"There must've been a Continental garrison in this neighborhood."

Sara blinked fearing the empty sidewalk was a slight trick of her mind but to her relief, it was not. All the ghosts were gone. The normal color slowly returned to her face as the fear that possessed for the last few minutes faded. Sarah pulled the shade down. Her heart pulsed causing rapid beats of terror, as she was still fearful that this orchestra would make a return appearance. She avoided looking at her husband. On some level, she felt embarrassed that she behaved not as a Naval officer should but instead as if she were a mere terrified little girl.

Without her needing to say anything, Alberto ran his fingers along Sarah's long black hair. She hummed. After what they experienced, it felt very soothing. The remainders of her shame disappeared and her husband's presence at her side made the last remnants of her fear evaporate. "What're, I mean, why've these ghosts come here?" She asked.

"They must've all been on patrol to protect the neighborhood from the British," Alberto replied. "Their actions are most honorable. In their death they've continued to uphold the oath they swore in life."

"Have you seen them before?"

"No, Sarah, I've not."

8.

The next morning Alberto and Sarah sat at the Arturo's kitchen table eating breakfast with Alberto's parents. At her core, Sarah was possessed by a fear that the otherworldly specters, which strolled outside last night, would return. As she sat there playing the role of the dutiful wife and daughter-in-law, she struggled to comprehend how such an event could scientifically occur. Alberto occasionally stroked her cheeks. Unknown to her, Alberto continued to wonder why the events of last night triggered a very distant memory.

Helena looked at her visitors from where she and Peter sat on the other side of the table. "I'm sorry you two were caught in the storm last night," she confessed. "How did you and Sarah sleep?" Helena asked her son.

"We slept well, Mother," Alberto answered. "But we heard some very loud noises coming from the street last night."

Peter stared across the table in concern. "What time last night did you hear this noise, son?" he probed. "And what did you hear?"

"It was just before midnight, my father, and it was music, Father, it was music that we heard."

Helena glared at her son while she sipped her morning tea. "We've heard it as well," she responded, "and we've heard it at some time for the last few nights."

"How long have you heard this noise, Mother?"

"It's a recent occurrence," Helena replied. "We've only heard this music for three nights now."

Alberto was silent for a few seconds as he considered the information recently provided to him by his mother. "Mother, Father, why didn't you tell me or Sarah about this music when we arrived last night?"

"We didn't think it would return," Peter stated. "Besides, we didn't think you could hear it over the storm."

9.

On Monday night, Sarah and Alberto lay under the sheets covering their makeshift bunk in the Arturo's living room after attending the first day of the historical conference. Sarah read a romance novel. As she lay beside her husband, the words on the page failed to fully occupy her mind, because her fears finally defeated her efforts through the day to control them, forcing their way to the surface. The clock ticked. Taken by surprise Sarah dropped her novel on the floor. In response, Alberto closed the historical journal he was reading to tend to his wife. "What's wrong Sarah?" he inquired. "Why've you become so terrified?

"I'm deeply troubled, Alberto," Sarah admitted, "that we'll again hear the unnatural production we heard last night."

"We'll just have to wait and see if it or those undead veterans make a return appearance."

Then from outside the Arturo's residence she heard a tune that compelled her to gaze towards the window against her will. "It's music," she whispered. "It's music I'm hearing."

"I hear it also," Alberto responded. "It sounds very familiar."

"It's those drum beats," Sarah panicked. "It's what we heard last night."

Sarah kissed her husband before leaving the foldout mattress and heading to the living room window because she knew she must investigate this orchestral playing for her own state of mind.

A few seconds later, Alberto rose from the mattress knowing that as Sarah's husband he possessed a duty to protect her and guard her from anything that might harm her and on this night that included her fears regarding this eerie drumbeat. Soon he was where he belonged, standing at his wife's side to act as her valiant guardian. He heard nothing from Sarah. Thus, his strong hand placed itself on her shoulder turning her towards him finding tears of terror dripping down her cheeks. "Sarah, what's wrong?" Alberto inquired.

"The musical instruments, my husband," Sarah gasped. "I fear they and the undead Continentals have returned but I don't dare find out if that's so."

"Why, Sarah?"

"I'm too terrified to confirm if my fears are true."

"You must face your fears." Out of a sense of duty to

his wife, Alberto pulled on the rod letting the shade rise exposing the sidewalk. Through the glass, Sarah and Alberto observed two groups of figures, which were moving in unison, and they knew they were the same shadows of Continental regulars they witnessed last night.

Sarah's eyes gazed through them. It was only a few seconds before her crying continued, this time releasing tears of great sadness. "Close it, Alberto!" she sobbed. "It's them; I've seen enough."

Alberto heeded his wife's request and released his grip on the cord letting it come down blocking the sidewalk. Sarah's lips trembled while the orchestra continued and in desperation she moved closer to her husband whose fingers moved along her side reassuring her that she was still safe. As he did, Alberto succeeded in long last remembering whom it was that once told him about this symphony all those many years ago. "I never believed him," Alberto confessed. "I never believed his claims about the music."

Sarah stared at her husband in puzzlement. "You told me last night was the first time you ever saw those figures. Did you lie to me, husband?"

"Everything I told you last night was true, Sarah," Alberto replied. "However, someone told me about the music a long time ago."

"When was it?"

"In my childhood."

"Who was it, Alberto?"

"It was Colonel Conway."

"Who is he, Alberto?"

"He was our neighbor when I was a child. The Colonel was a veteran of the Second World War just as my father was but he was a Marine. At times, he claimed to hear a strange chorus being played outside during the night."

"Did you believe him?"

"As a child I thought the Colonel was simply conjuring ghost stories to amuse and frighten all of the children in the neighborhood, including me. After the last two nights I wonder if, the instruments those undead minstrels played were the source of the music Colonel Conway once claimed to have been torment by at night."

In accordance with the duty he swore to perform for the rest of his life, Alberto remained by his wife's side as the music continued outside for a few more minutes. The clock chimed the hour. Now it was midnight and as occurred last night, the music ended. More tears escaped from Sarah's eyes.

Sensing how truly upset and terrified she was, Alberto pulled the woman he loved close to him and lowered her face into his muscular chest. In these long few minutes following midnight, Sarah let herself melt into her husband's body, seeking the security that only he could provide her because all of her confidence was washed away, reducing her to a very terrified woman.

"There... There, Sarah," Alberto whispered. "It's all right. I'm here."

Sarah continued crying until all the tears were gone.

"You don't need to be afraid, Sarah," Alberto spoke. "I'm here and I'll always be here for you."

"Thank you for being here to protect me, my love."

"Do you feel better now?"

"Yes, Alberto, I do."

10.

The next morning Sarah and Alberto sat at the kitchen table finishing breakfast with Peter and Helena. As Sarah sat there, a slight tremble in her wrist from the lingering terror, she sought to suppress her trauma, as it would be undignified to let it be detected by her in-laws.

Across from her, Peter put his bagel down his plate. "I've heard many rumors over the years about historic Philadelphia," he uttered. "It has been said the dead walk the streets there during the day and haunt it at night."

For the sake of his wife, Alberto chose to respond to his father. "We walked through historic Philadelphia during the conference's lunch break, Father," he claimed. "We didn't see any ghosts, just tourists walking through the graveyards."

Helena lowered her teacup onto the coaster. There was something she could no longer avoid admitting to her son and her daughter-in-law. "Alberto, I've been worried about you and Sarah," she admitted. "I hope you slept better last night."

"We heard that music again, Mother," Alberto informed her. "Could you or Father hear any of it?"

"We didn't hear anything last night, Alberto. The cotton balls we purchased yesterday to wear in our ears at night very thankfully blocked all of it out."

Sarah's eyes blinked as she was pondering her mother-in-law's statement. Then a faint smile emerged on her face because it gave her an idea, which she felt must be implemented without too much of a delay. "Alberto, we shouldn't come straight back to your parents house after the conference ends," she explained. "Instead, we're going to purchase something so we don't hear the music again tonight."

11.

As the clock on the leaving room table ticked away, Alberto and Sarah lay under the sheets on the third night of their visit. Both of them wore earmuffs. They were purchased at a local store, to silence the mysterious and terrifying performances that seemed to appear late at night signifying the return of the undead patriots and their accompanying performers. With his right hand, Alberto gently tapped his wife's shoulders. In response, Sarah raised her ear earmuffs, to hear what her husband needed to say to her. "What's wrong, my love?" she asked.

"The hour of midnight approaches," Alberto

explained. "Do you hear anything?"

"I only hear you and the clock, husband. Beyond that I hear nothing else."

With that statement, Sarah pulled the earmuffs back over her ears and returned to her novel. Alberto did the same in a few seconds. As her eyes scanned the page, she listened to the night for one last time and to her immense satisfaction heard nothing as the clock chimed the start of the new day.

Sarah smiled. She was very happy to be free from the ever-present instrumental cadence made by long deceased balladeers, which foretold the coming of phantoms of once living Continental regulars whose presence previously disturbed their slumber.

This was now the first night since the couple arrived in Philadelphia, on which their sleep would not be interrupted by the peculiar events happening outside, which suited both Sarah and Alberto just fine.

december

'Twas the Night
Jennifer DiMarco

'Twas the night before Christmas and all through the house
not a creature was stirring, not even a mouse.
The stockings were hung by the chimney with care,
in hopes that Saint Nicholas soon would be there.
Our children were nestled, all snug in their beds
while visions of morning danced in their heads.
And Momma in her 'kerchief, and I in my cap,
had just settled our brains for a long winter's nap—
when out on the lawn there arose such a clatter!
I sprang from our bed to see what was the matter.

I ran to the window and threw up the sash,
searching for danger, perhaps being rash.
The moon on the breast of the new-fallen snow,
gave a luster of midday to objects below.
But day it was not, and dawn is not promised;
the beauty was cold, if I had to be honest.
I turned from the window to return to my bed
when the curtains they billowed, filling with dread.

Into the room, a bitter wind moaned
and through the night's veil, a darkness was sown.
I heard my wife whisper: "Papa, beware."
as silence fell eerie, thick with despair.

Back to the vista, my eyes they did search,
for the wind was too bitter—not of this Earth.
"Look," said my wife, coming to stand
there at my side and taking my hand.
I followed her gaze to the edge of our land
where a forest primeval towered so grand.
From deep in that darkness, they slowly appeared:
bodies like scorpions, heads like reindeer.
They walked in an arrow, as if stalking a hunt.
Red blood dripped from the beast in the front.

Across moonlit snow they left nary a print;
only scurries of spiders gave any dark hint
that walking among them, so tall and so thin
with eyes empty midnight and continence grim,
was he who most humans never will see.
(Not see and survive, for no one can flee.)
It was there on the lawn, the master took pause
with fingers like talons and mouth like a maw.
His presence so powerful, he'd stolen our breath,
I knew in that moment, I was looking at Death.

Impatient, the beasts, they clawed at the land.
His coursers, they reared when they heard his command:
 "Now, Dasher! Now, Demon! Now, Profit and Vixen!

On, Comet! On, Cain! On, Damian and Blitzen!
Surround these four souls! Surround these four walls!
Keep them and hold them. Encircle them all!"

As leaves that before the wild hurricane fly,
when they meet with an obstacle mount to the sky,
so to the air, the coursers they flew
and settled around the only home that we knew.
They created a circle, sealed with their ill;
if we tried to get out, we'd surely be killed.
Next, in a moment as fast as a shot,
Death stood in the moonlight... and then he was not!

In slow motion (at least), I turned from the view
when downstairs I heard him, and my lady did, too.
He sounded like snakes, an unending hiss.
He walked through our walls, a living abyss.
From the top of the stairs, between him and the kids,
we stood and we watched him—goodness forbid!
When he came to our tree, strung with bright lights,
he threw back his head and laughed at our plight.

His eyes—how they burned! His face made me wary;
his cheeks cracked with cackles. He knew what he carried:
Plucked from his flesh, like burrs from his back—
the wares from a peddler with hell in his pack.

The gifts, like him, were not of this Earth,
but objects of dread, of despair, and of dearth.
A mirror that showed not your face but your fears!

A clock that ticked backward, unraveling years!
A jar full of whispers, voicing dark rages!
A book with no story, just endless sharp pages!
Why had we not feared, each year with this rite,
to welcome inside all that is bright?
Had we not worried, that one winter night
the thing that would come, would arrive with a bite?

"No plums or fairies,
no candies or berries,
no treasures or toys
for good girls and boys."
We stood and we watched and we knew it was true
those free-of-care nights were definitely through.
As we heard Death intone his insidious rhyme
our innocence shriveled and died on the vine.
Never again could we open our home
lest something creep in with a chill for our bones.

But as quick as he came—the Grim—he was gone,
leaving before the first light of dawn.
We looked at each other—Momma and me—
we checked on our children, still weak in the knees.
The house was so quiet, all wrapped up in fear.
Proof that evil had been nearer than near.
Back at our window like moths we were drawn
to stand side by side and peer out at the lawn.

There stood the phantom, the specter, the Fate.
While his scorpion-deer still circled in wait.

Then a pulse on the air marked their dismissal
and they gathered around him like thorns on a thistle.
We hid and we watched the demons et al
return to the wilderness like after the Fall.

This night was different from every other.
We huddled in bed and held one another.
I never thought to dispose of the gifts.
Just tossed and turned, afraid of what-ifs.
But when morning broke, the day was the same.
The children were laughing, unwrapping their games.
The mirror, the clock, the jar and the book?
Not to be found; trust me, did I look!
Those darkest of talismans with intentions so stark
hid in the daylight and only thrived in the dark.

Sometimes, past midnight, when my family's asleep
I'll see the book or the clock and quietly weep.
A reminder that nothing is just what it seems.
That nightmares are real and walk out of dreams.
What if the jar sends out a squall?
And the beasts with their master answer the call?
What if the mirror shows me his face
and my heart misses beats and loses its pace?
Every new winter when Christmas draws near
I think of those tokens, that night full of fear.
For beneath all the joy, all the laughter and light,
lurks Death with a whisper, "And to all, a still night."

thirteen

Otis

Marshall Miller

ome on, Frank. It's just an elevator ride."

"Jim, it's a dammed ride in a glass elevator to the top of the Space Needle."

"So? It's perfectly safe. I bet you it's an Otis or one based on those designs."

"What has that got to do with it, Jim? It's still a glass elevator with most of the passenger area covered in glass. It makes it look like it's open completely."

"So? What's the issue here?" "Jim was becoming very exasperated with his co-worker.

"I told you, " replied Frank. "I have a phobia—"

"With elevators?"

Frank took a deep breath and tried not to start yelling. He was becoming so exasperated to have to explain his paralyzing phobia, however, once more into the breach to satisfy his co-worker.

"It's called Acrophobia. It's an extreme fear of heights or situations that involve exposure to places resembling tall heights. It is a mental health condition that is a type of anxiety disorder."

"Yeah? Well, how did you become—infected—with this disorder?"

"How to begin?" thought Frank. Should he try to explain the nasty falls he took as a child? How about when he was five years old and at a great uncle's house under construction, he opened a door and—surprise!—no stairs. Luckily, the floor below was still just unfinished sand. Or when he was punished for pushing his sister off a bridge for teasing him? It was a low bridge and no broken bones, but it affected his young psyche. And now, some situations push the extreme fear buttons, often leading to freezing in place.

"Look it, Jim. Lots of things happened when I was very young. It's all psychological imprinting that I have been unable to get rid of as I grew older." Frank pointed to the offending elevator. "That thing is a big trigger."

Jim grunted before he replied, "Well, the bosses are having lunch in the Space Needle Lounge in your honor. You are the hero of the moment for defeating that multimillion-dollar suit against our largest client. Proving the claims were fraudulent through your investigation is a major feather in the corporate hat."

"I know, Jim, it's just—"

"Look it, Frank. You can shut your eyes, and I'll ride with you. I'll hold your hands if you want me. It's not a long elevator ride."

Frank was sweating at the idea of stepping into

the elevator.

"We wait, Frank, until the two of us are the only passengers. I'll keep you from falling anywhere." Jim paused, then added, "But you really need to seek some psychological help."

Frank took a large breath to calm down. He saw no winning tactic other than acquiesce to Jim. "Well, we can try. It would be much easier if my phobia were spiders, like Ellen."

Jim laughed as he took Frank by his arm. "Yeah, she runs, screaming at the sight of a tiny spider. Now, close your eyes. I lead you into the elevator; you keep your eyes shut tight until I tell you to open them. Okay?"

"Okay," Frank replied shakily.

About a minute later, Jim led Frank into the elevator. "Stand here, Frank. The button is being pushed. Up we go with eyes shut."

Frank kept his eyes squeezed tight as he felt the elevator moving. "Let me know when I can open my eyes, Jim."

Silence.

"Jim?"

The elevator jerked to a stop.

"Jim!"

Frank reached out and felt—no one.

He screamed as his testicles tried to retreat up into his body.

Frank squeezed his eyes as tight as possible. Shear

panic descended as his animal mind told him he would fall from the elevator. Frank began to quiver and shake.

The lawyer did not know how long his mind was controlled by unreasoned panic, but he eventually formed the thought to feel for the emergency telephones all elevators had. Still keeping his eyes squeezed shut so hard that they were beginning to ache, he held the phone handset to his ear. Eventually, a female voice stated, "Monitor Control. Are you having a problem in the Space Needle elevator?"

"I'm stuck! I'm here all alone! I—"

"Sir, can you take a deep breath and calm down? I can see you on the connected elevator security camera. You are in no danger of falling. The glass exterior is undamaged—"

"*I'm going to fall!*" Frank screamed. His eyes popped open and focused on the height of the elevator. Frank shrieked and collapsed onto the floor of the elevator. His bladder control failed, and he wet himself.

"Sir, you are in no danger of injury. Help is on the way. We are attempting to put the elevator back into operation. I will stay on the phone until you get out of the elevator. Okay?"

Frank voiced an unintelligible string of noises, followed by sobbing.

"Sir, can you give me your name? Sir?"

Eventually, Frank responded."Frank Stiles."

"Well, Mister Stiles, help is on the way. Technicians are working on getting the elevator operating once more.

Please remain calm. You are in no danger of falling. All elevators have safety systems developed originally by Otis Elevator, preventing them from falling to the ground."

Frank sobbed.

Frank screamed when the elevator jerked, seemed to fall a few feet, and then shuddered again to a stop.

"Mister Stiles? The elevator moved as technicians were working on its operation. It is in no danger of falling—"

The elevator dropped a foot, and Frank screamed incoherently as his bowels let loose.

A few moments later, the elevator began an accelerated trip upward to the Space Needle Lounge. When it jerked to a stop, and the doors opened, Frank tumbled out of the elevator and began to vomit.

The law firm gave Frank an extra week of paid leave and picked up the tab for some top-rate psychological counseling for his phobia. Frank did admit he had nightmares of falling regularly. People made jokes about Frank falling out of the elevator and puking for weeks. Jealousy for the new 'Hero of the Office' often ran deep.

It was leaked to Frank that Jim thought it was a big joke to put Frank in the elevator and step out at the last moment. Jim apologized for the attempt at a joke that had backfired during a meeting with the senior partner and the Human Resources manager. Frank grudgingly accepted his apology and returned to work, putting the incident behind him. A cash settlement helped.

Two weeks later, a masked man in a jumpsuit hit Jim in the groin with a baseball while entering his car at the parking garage.

After the incident, Jim had severe fears of impotence and erectile dysfunction, which led to a divorce and alcoholism.

Ellen the Arachnophobe quit as her office seemed to be a new meeting place for giant spiders.

Other people in the law firm soon had bouts with their often-hidden phobias. The worst case was when Dave Jones ran out screaming when a crowd of clowns showed up with all their slap-stick schticks. It turned out Dave had a severe reaction to clowns because of some abuse in his childhood.

These fear-based incidents at first seemed random. Then, people began questioning whether one person was behind all this strife. Maybe some former client or adversary of the law firm held a grudge?

Frank used the settlement money to strike out on his own. He specialized in cases involving office harassment and emotional distress. The firm was soon a resounding success, with Frank Stiles opening it on the ground floor of a new office building.

On his desk at his firm were two plaques. The first read, "Fear and phobia are not laughing matters."

The second plaque read, "Payback's a bitch."

author biographies

JANUARY

Bree Indigo is a poet and songwriter. She enjoys tarot, exploring Washington State's Olympic Peninsula, and tending to her menagerie of pets. She has been published in all five volumes of *Unnerving* and all three volumes of the women's poetry and essay collection, *Rise*. Indigo lives with her wife and their family in the Puget Sound. Her first memoir, *Unreliable Narrator*, is forthcoming from Blue Forge Press. Find her on Instagram @bree_indigo

FEBRUARY

Dakoda Foxx is a writer, actor, artist, and paralegal. She is dedicated to making a positive impact on the people she comes in contact with. She advocates for people's rights and dedicates her life to help make a change for others. She hopes her readers see that there is light at the end of any tunnel, in any situation. Dakoda's memoir, *The Magic in the Nightmare that was Me*, is a story of survival, perserverance, and a spirit that refused to be broken. She has also written a pocket-sized book in the *Haunting of Orchard House* series called *Paranoia* and has contributed to the *Rise* poetry & short story collections *Resurrection (Volume 2)* and *Revolution (Volume 3)*. Dakoda's books are available at www.BlueForgePress.com. Find her on Facebook at: https://www.facebook.com/DakodaFoxxAuthorPage

MARCH

Pauline Ugalde is a visually-impaired writer, gamer, amateur musician, and voice-actor. Her favorite genres are sci-fi, fantasy, and horror, and her creative influences are Stephen King, Mark Z. Danielewski, Toby Fox, and Daniel Mullins. Her favorite scary movie is *Get Out*.

APRIL

Avery Kellam likes to explore that razor-line between darkness and sex, with themes of fantasy and monsters that are exquisitely tantalizing and filled with torture. She dives into the second circle of hell for her characters, and brings them into the light for all to enjoy.

MAY

Sami Ridge is a multi-disciplinary artist living in Seattle. Before migrating up the Pacific Coast, she became a published poet, having received first place in the Ina Coolbrith Circle Poets' Dinner Award (Nature Category), among others. In 2021 she released her first of two music singles to critical acclaim. Recently, she co-curated Stone Pacific zines 8th issue. She now splits her time between art modeling, painting, song & screenwriting, with the intent to release her first E.P., and take on her first film acting role, in the coming year. All of this can be watched from her Instagram, @samiridge

JUNE

Author, illustrator, and award-winning actor and filmmaker, Maxwell DiMarco has been writing professionally since he was a pre-teen, with stories and novels published in *Tales of the Slug, Super,* and *Ghost Sniffers, Inc.* He has also written for every volume of *Unnerving,* where he explores the darker aspects of society through physical and psychological horror. DiMarco lives in the Pacific Northwest, where he works as a special effects editor and is the host of the weekly children's series, *Seriously Cereal.* He is a huge believer in community, acceptance, and seeing the world from all perspectives, striving to always provide his readers with an intriguing, thought-provoking narrative, no matter the genre.

JULY

Michelle Lee is a Pacific Northwest native with an imagination open to possibilities. In her downtime, Michelle is an avid reader, loves to explore different areas in the northwest, speaks fluent sarcasm, and enjoys spending time with her significant other and their two cats. She loves to hear from readers and can be found on Facebook and Instagram.

AUGUST

Joe Nasta (ze/zir) is a queer multimodal artist and writer who works in Seattle. Ze is one half of the art and poetry collective Eat Yr Manhood and head curator of Stone Pacific Zine. Zir work has been published in The Rumpus, Occulum, Peach Mag, Yes Poetry, dream boy book club, and others. Joe's first book of poetry "I want you to feel ugly, too" came out in 2021.

SEPTEMBER

Living in the PNW, there is plenty to do to get to the great outdoors. Marie Locker's outdoorsy lifestyle includes photography and camping—or rather, glamping—with her three kids, husband, a dog and a cat. She loves wine, horror movies, and anything spooky.

OCTOBER

Hailing from Tacoma, WA, Lauren Patzer has been an information technology guru, actor, writer and film producer among other pursuits. His love of horror began with a non-stop reading of *The Amityville Horror*. With two novels and over fifty short stories published now, his most recent work is the horror novel *Undead Reckoning*.

NOVEMBER

Daniel DiQuinzio is a freelance writer living in New Jersey. Born mentally and physically disabled, he holds a Master of Arts degree in history from Seton Hall University. He is a contributor to *Veteran Voices Newsletter*, *Marjorie Magazine*, and *Palm Coast Magazine*. His fiction has also appeared in *Real Love Magazine*, *Bohemian Renaissance*, *Urban Tymes*, *Sisyphus Quarterly*, *The Minority Report* and in *Naughty & Nice: Stories for Your Stocking*. DiQuinzio's poetry has appeared in *Sisyphus Quarterly*, *Sherlock Holmes Mystery Magazine*, and *Neurocentrikk* and his nonfiction has appeared in *Philadelphia Row Home*, *Palm Coast Magazine* and *New Jersey Monthly*.

DECEMBER

A PNWC and Bumbershoot award-winning poet and Seattle Times bestselling novelist, Jennifer DiMarco first toured nationally as an author when she was nineteen years old, having written novels since the age of ten. The first sixteen years of her career included the publication of contemporary drama, high fantasy, science fiction, poetry, and mystery novels as well as the production of two short films and three stage plays. During a twenty-year hiatus from prose, DiMarco married, raised two children, and worked as a filmmaker writing and directing more than a dozen feature films, half a dozen mini series, and more than a hundred short films. She returned to prose with *Hannah at Night and Twelve Other Stories* in 2020. DiMarco lives in the Pacific Northwest with her wife, composer and actor Brianne, and their adult children, author and illustrator Maxwell, and actor and illustrator Faith.

THIRTEEN

Marshall Miller retired from Homeland Security and police enforcement to more deeply explore the human condition and what drives us a species. Framed with the arrival of alien Apex predators who see us as little more than a food source, Miller is best known for crafting his series, *The Tschaaa Infestation* that dares to ask: Are we truly superior and do we deserve to survive? Find out more about his work at www.tiny.cc/marshallmiller